NOW THAT I *found you*

A HEART'S COMPASS BOOK FOUR

USA TODAY BESTSELLING AUTHOR

BROOKE O'BRIEN

NOW THAT I FOUND YOU

All I ever wanted was a family of my own.

Loss and heartbreak taught me not to wish for something that could so easily be ripped away.

Until Callum.

It wasn't until I fell in love and married him I found myself wishing for the life I thought was always out of reach.

Life always has a way of testing us. Anything can be stolen from you in a second—I know this better than anyone.

When one man threatens to rip everything away from me again, I'll be forced to fight.

For Callum, for us, and for the future we both want...

Thank you for reading **NOW THAT I FOUND YOU**! I hope you love catching up with Callum and Ellie's as much as I did.

You can join my Facebook group, Brooke O'Brien's Rebel Reader Group, to discuss the series and get sneak peeks on future releases. Sign up for my newsletter to find out more about my new releases. To join, visit: www.authorbrookeobrien.com/follow.

Enjoy!

READING ORDER

WHERE I FOUND YOU

a small town, on the run, secret identify romantic suspense

LOST BEFORE YOU

a small town meets big city, friends to lovers romance

UNTIL I FOUND YOU

a small town, second chance romance

NOW THAT I FOUND YOU

an emotional and gripping surprise pregnancy, romantic suspense

WHERE YOU BELONG

a single parent, law enforcement, small town romance

Learn more and purchase your copy at:
www.authorbrookeobrien.com/heartscompass

dedication

This book is dedicated to anyone who's ever struggled to let go of their past and find the love they deserve. I hope you'll always remember...

You are strong.

You are beautiful.

You are enough.

prologue

ELLIE

I've always believed the people we grow into are a result of the challenges we've faced and the lessons we've learned throughout our lives. The decisions we make guide us down different paths, leading us to destinations we had never planned or expected for ourselves. While there's always a little bit of God's hand and fate at play, it's ultimately our decisions that lead us to where we end up.

I still remember the day I met Callum, standing outside the bus station in the pouring rain. The heartbreak I had lived through leading me to make the difficult decision to leave my small town of Garwood. It was one of many choices I had been forced to make at such a young age.

I fell for him all over again the night at Brodie's when I saw the sparkle in his eye and the rebellious grin he wore on his face. He made it so hard for me to stay away from him, even though I knew the risks of letting him in.

I know with all my heart he was brought into my life with the purpose of showing me there are people in this world who will protect me and love me, scars and all. Marrying him was the best decision I've ever made in my life. When I stop and allow myself to think about it, I smile knowing my dad had a hand in bringing Callum to me.

I found a family here in Arbor Creek and a place I can finally call home. For the first time, I'm allowing myself to picture a life I never thought I could have. One that I always thought was out of reach for me.

All I've ever wanted was a family of my own. But like everything in my life, I should've known the road ahead wasn't going to be easy for the two of us. Life has always had its way of testing me. Our future is about to change in ways we never expected, and one man's decisions threaten to take everything I've always wanted away from me again.

chapter one

CALLUM
august

"You almost ready, baby?" I ask, as I lightly tap my knuckles on the door. Leaning in closer, I listen for signs of movement on the other side.

The sound of Ellie's heels clicking on the tile floor of our hotel suite brings a smile to my face. Just the mental image of seeing her in her summer dress, getting ready, knowing how beautiful she looks.

Running my hand over my button-up shirt, I step back when I hear the footsteps approaching before the door handle is turned and she's standing before me.

Her hair has a light wave to it, brighter than it was just a week ago. Her tan skin is bronzer and there's a light dusting of freckles appearing over the apples of her cheeks. They are rosy from the sun she got when we were lying out on the beach earlier today.

Glancing down, I take in my wife standing in front of me. She looks like a fucking angel in her white dress. It cuts into a deep V, teasing me with what I know she looks like underneath.

Following the path down to her legs to the heels wrapped around her feet, I barely hold back the urge to drop to my knees before her. She's a fucking sight to see. The possessive side of me wants to growl, pull her into my arms, and keep her locked away in our hotel room for the rest of the night.

I don't know how I got so lucky with her, but I won't let her know I question it either. When I see the glistening of the wedding band flashing where it sits on her ring finger, something in me shifts.

She's my wife and despite hating the thought of any other man looking at her, I love knowing she's wearing my ring and showing the world she's mine. That's enough to get me to let go of my overprotectiveness and instead, reach out and grab her hand, pulling her closer to me.

"I'm ready." She giggles, as she falls against my chest. She rubs her palm over my abs, biting her lip as she peers up at me.

"Don't look at me like that, Ellie."

There's a sparkle in her eye at my comment as a light smirk lines her lips. It distracts me, I swear she leaves me constantly hanging on the edge with want. I could so easily close the distance between us and kiss her mouth.

"Like what?" She feigns innocence, which on any other day I might actually believe, but right now, I know better.

Her tongue darts out, lightly tracing a line over her lip, teasing me. She knows exactly what she's doing. It can't happen right now though. We have a dinner reservation in ten minutes, and I have plans for her, despite how good she looks right now.

"Don't think I don't see through that innocent look, sweetheart. I know you better than that," I growl, kissing her deeply. She hums softly, as she slides her hands up my chest and around my neck, holding me close to her.

I love how confident she's become around me. The once shy and timid girl, held back by her past, doesn't hold herself back anymore. She takes what she wants, and I love how she doesn't suppress her urges when it's me she wants.

Keeping my forehead pressed against hers, I break our kiss and struggle to breathe again.

"We have dinner reservations at eight o'clock. We should get going. If I don't stop us now, we will end up like last night where I'm ordering you room service and feeding you dinner in bed naked again."

She smiles deviously before she nods her head. "We are on our honeymoon after all."

For a minute I think she's ready for me to cancel our plans before she pulls back, lacing her fingers in mine. "We might as well enjoy it while we can. We're married now, which means we'll have many days of naked dinners when we're back home."

I almost consider saying to hell with it, when she turns and pulls me down the hallway of our hotel suite. I get a glimpse of her in this dress from behind, her hair pulled over to the side, showing off the column of her neck, making my cock twitch in my pants.

"Fuck," I mutter to myself, as she squeezes my hand tighter as she looks back at me, biting her lip.

"Let's make this quick then."

Once we're out of the hotel and heading down toward the beach, I'm glad we decided to keep our plans for the evening. The sun has started to set, lighting up the sky in a beautiful array of pink and orange, as the waves crash in the distance. We make it to the end of the dock, leading us to the secluded area I had arranged for us for tonight.

Ellie stops, leaning down to undo the strap around her foot before I bend down in front of her. Unhooking the clasp, I ease her foot out of her heels as she steps down into the sand.

I probably should've asked you if my shoes were appropriate for tonight," she whispers down to me.

Running my hand over her calf down to her ankle, I peer up at her and smile. "Oh, they're always appropriate. I'll show you why later."

She grins, shaking her head at me. "Lord, what am I going to do with you?"

"I can think of a few things." I chuckle.

"Mhmm." She laughs, as I lead her over to the blanket laid out in the sand overlooking the water. When she sees the setup I had arranged for her, she lets out a subtle gasp before she wraps her arms around my waist.

"Callum," she sighs. "I can't believe..." Her voice drifts off, as she looks down at the flowers, along with the picnic basket.

"You did all of this?"

I nod. "Of course, I did."

She rises up onto her toes, and I lean forward, pressing a kiss against her lips. "Thank you."

I've always loved how easy it is to surprise Ellie. She is grateful for every ounce of love you show her, eager to soak it up. It only makes me want to find new ways to express how I feel for her, wanting to put the same look of love and appreciation on her face every day.

She steps back as I lower myself to the ground, helping her down between my legs. Wrapping my arms around her, pulling her close, she reclines against my chest.

"It's so beautiful here, so peaceful," she sighs blissfully, and I'd give anything to grant her this sense of calmness everyday of our lives. She deserves all the happiness in the world.

I nod. "It's everything I hoped it would be for you."

Leaning over, I pull the basket closer to us. Reaching in, I grab the sandwiches I had packed away earlier when Ellie was taking a nap. We sit here, our bodies entwined, eating as we reminisce over our week. Most of our time was spent tangled up together in our room or somewhere near the water.

"I'm not sure I'm ready to leave yet. Can't we just stay here forever?" Ellie murmurs. She shifts her eyes downcast, tossing her napkin back into the basket. I help her clean up everything before she moves to situate herself back in my arms again.

"We still have the rest of the night here. We might as well enjoy what time we have left."

Tilting my head forward, I press a kiss against her shoulder. She's soft and warm from her sunburn, heat radiating from her skin. The moment my lips brush against her, I feel her body tremble beneath my touch.

I've always loved the way she reacts to me. Tracing my tongue over her shoulder, I kiss her again from the base of her neck up toward her jaw.

"Callum," she breathes. Her hands grip my arms tightly, holding me to her.

"Yes, sweetheart?"

She doesn't say anything, the words falling the moment they touch her lips coming out more like a small hiss, just as I press another kiss beneath her ear.

She tilts her head to the side, giving me better access to her, and I dive right in. Her chest rises and falls heavily with each forced breath.

Reaching my hand up beneath the curve of her breast, she rests her head back against my shoulder as my finger brushes over her nipple beading through the chiffon of her dress.

"Oh, God," she whispers. She quickly checks around us, making sure we're still alone.

"No one's here, Ellie, but us. Just you and me. I'd never share you with anyone."

She lets out an audible breath, relaxing again in my arms. She's telling me without words she wants me to continue, and I do.

"Does that feel good?" I exhale against her cheek.

She nods, her tongue darting out, wetting her lips. She uncrosses her legs, leaving them stretched out in front of us. I brush my other hand over her stomach, down to the apex of her thigh, pulling the hem of her dress up enough for me to slip my hand beneath the material.

Her body shutters beneath me as I skim the tip of my finger over the seam of her panties, feeling her wetness seep through.

"Damn, sweetheart," I groan, pressing my mouth against her shoulder once again.

Slipping my finger inside her panties, she lets her leg fall open for me. My cock aches in my pants by how bad she wants this right now. My finger grazes over her swollen clit and she doesn't hold back, unleashing a breathy moan.

I alternate between rubbing her clit, to grazing the edge of her pussy lips, before she begs me to stop teasing her. She shifts her head back, her eyes meeting mine, and I see the hunger in the depths. My girl needs me to give her this and, God, I want to give her everything she wants and so much more.

"C'mere," I mutter, urging her to turn to face me. Her movements are slow, her eyes in a daze, as I quickly unzip my pants. My cock rejoices when I wrap my hand around it, pumping it once, twice.

Her eyes laser into me and what I'm doing. I reach for her, needing to feel her body against mine, when she hesitates for a minute.

"I want to watch you do that," she breathes, sliding her hand between her legs to touch herself. Good lord, she is fucking perfect.

I give her what she wants, rubbing my thumb over the tip of my dick, catching the cum dripping before reaching out and pressing it against her lips. She opens her mouth for me, tasting me, as her eyes light up with fire in the depths.

She ditches her earlier idea and closes the distance between us, rubbing her wetness over me, coating my cock. She pulls her panties to the side as she moves to slide down over me, keeping me pressed to the hilt.

Her eyes find mine again, and the love I find shining back at me is nearly my undoing. The way she fits so perfectly around me makes my heart beat out of my chest. Having her body pressed against me, it's as if everything makes sense. I'm whole.

Her fingers run through my hair, pulling on the strands as she tilts my head back and captures my lips in a soul-crushing kiss. Her body rocks against mine as my hands wrap tightly around her waist, holding her to me.

She throws her head back. Leaning my head forward, I kiss her neck, feeling her heart beat beneath my lips through every struggled breath she takes.

"Callum," she moans, her grip on my hair tightens, and I know she's close. Her body is wound so tight as her pussy clenches around me.

"Ellie, baby. I want you to come with me. Come, baby," I mutter, just as I lightly bite down on her collarbone.

Her body trembles, as she wraps her arms around my neck collapsing against me. I wrap my arms around her. She doesn't move to break our connection, only moves to circle her legs around my lower back, holding herself closer to me.

When our heart rates both go back to normal, I reach my hand up and brush my thumb over the apple of her cheek as I whisper, "I swear you were made to be loved by me."

chapter two

ELLIE

I ended up sleeping most of the flight home. When Callum woke me, he told me he had been trying to wake me up since the flight attendants announced we were preparing for landing.

We arrive at the Des Moines airport, about forty minutes away from Arbor Creek. Callum left his truck parked at the airport so once we collect our luggage, we're back on the road and heading home. I turn my phone back on, and I'm surprised when the pinging starts, signaling several messages from our friends and family. Callum's mom, Connie, has been eagerly waiting for us to tell her all about our trip, along with my best friends, Kinsley, Halle, and Brea.

The entire drive, I sit in the middle of the seat with my head on Callum's shoulder. His hand alternates between holding my thigh and steering. We sit in silence as every mile passes by bringing us closer to home.

"You doin' okay?" Callum questions, peering over to check my face before turning his attention back on the road. He presses a small kiss against my forehead as I curl my body into his side, wrapping my hand around his arm.

He reaches his hand down between us, wrapping his fingers in mine, pressing another kiss to the top and once more near the ring that sits on my finger.

My heart warms at how sweet he is, always finding little ways to remind me how much he loves me and wants to take care of me.

Tilting my head back, I glance up at him. "I think so, I just haven't been feeling well. I'm not sure if it's nerves from flying or if I'm coming down with something."

My stomach rolls, feeling the sudden nausea wash over me. The flight to Maui had been the first time I'd ever been on a plane, and I'm still suffering from jitters. Or it's jet lag. Either way, with the flight behind us, I'll be glad when we're finally home.

"I'm hurrying." He squeezes my hand reassuringly, as I nod my head getting comfortable again.

Callum wraps his hand around my knee, rubbing his thumb back and forth over the tan skin. I force all thoughts of not feeling well out of my head and think back on our honeymoon.

The entire week was like a dream. Callum, being the sweet man he is, planned everything. I think that's what made it even more special. All of the thought he put into every day we spent together. My favorite part, by far, was the day we went snorkeling, followed by a night under the stars as we had dinner on the beach.

"I know I've said this a hundred times over the past week but thank you. I can't get over how amazing everything from our wedding to the honeymoon was."

"Of course, baby." He leans forward, pressing a soft kiss against my lips.

When Callum asked me to marry him, I knew without a doubt there was no one else I'd ever want to spend forever with. He was it for me–the person I've been searching for all my life. When you've grown up like I have, you begin to think that love and marriage are not in the cards for you.

With the trial going on during the wedding planning process, it brought up a lot of emotions I had been working to bury after the assault. I was ready to move forward with my life but talking about the past resurfaced the grief of losing my dad and grandma, along with the sadness of what I thought my life would look like with my family.

Not many women can say that their husband, with the help of their best friend, planned most of their wedding. Callum promised to give me the wedding of my dreams. Honestly, I just wanted to marry him. I didn't care about having a big wedding, I just wanted to know he was my husband and to share the day with the people in our lives who mattered most to us.

"I'm ready for us to get home and start our life together."

"Me, too, sweetheart," he sighs. "I promise to spend the rest of my life making you happier than you ever thought possible."

Tears prick my eyes hearing the sincerity of his words as we both get lost staring out the window as the miles of highway pass us by. If there's anything in this world I know with absolute certainty, it's how much Callum Reid loves me. In the beginning, I resisted him and kept him at arm's length. I never wanted to accept that someone would love me and take care of me the way he wanted to. Now I cannot imagine my life without him, and I don't want to either.

I want to sigh when I spot our driveway coming over the hill. We pull up in front of the house, and Callum shifts the truck into park. Turning to face me, he runs his hand along my cheek up into my hair. His thumb brushes softly over my skin, sending shivers through me at his touch.

"I think I'm gonna go and lie down for a bit. I'm tired and not feeling the best. It's probably the time change and the traveling catching up to me."

"Of course, I don't mind," he whispers, pressing a kiss against my lips. He leans back, looking me in the eye, smiling as he touches his lips to mine again. "I'll get us unpacked and then I'll come in and lie down with you. I could use a nap myself."

I'm drifting off to sleep when I feel the bed move as Callum climbs in next to me, pulling me closer so that my body is molded with his. He presses a soft kiss against the curve where my neck meets my shoulder before whispering a soft, "I love you." My body relaxes, lulling me into a deep sleep.

I'm not sure what time it is when we both finally wake up, but the sun has since gone down. Callum moves to slip out of bed, jolting me from my sleep. He feels me move, stopping his movement and instead presses another kiss against my neck.

He's always loved kissing me there, and it's something I've come to crave from him. I moan softly feeling his breath feather across my skin. His lips cause goose bumps to break out over my skin, as I reach up holding his head close to me.

"You feelin' better now, baby?"

I nod my head, curving my lower back to press deeper into him. His hands wrapped around my middle, pull me in closer, forcing him to rub his length against my ass.

When one of his hands starts running along the edge of my pants, I turn my body, giving him better access to me. Curling my arm around the back of his head, he moans as I deepen the kiss.

Callum slips his hand beneath the waistband of my lounge pants. When he realizes I'm not wearing panties, he pulls back and glares at me with a hard stare.

"What's this?" he asks, running his hand over my smooth mound. I let my leg fall open for him.

"Ellie," Callum moans, as he moves his hand further south, his hand skimming over my pussy. My breath stutters, feeling my pelvis lift off the bed in search of his fingers.

"Greedy," he responds matter-of-factly.

"Callum," I groan, pulling the hair at the back of his head, kissing him forcefully. "Please," I whisper, begging him.

He moves between my legs, tossing the blanket that had been covering us to the side. There's a sparkle in his eye as he leans over me. Reaching for the waistband again, he pulls my pants down in one swift motion as he bites down on his lip to stifle his groan.

Sitting up, I stare down at my body following his line of sight, as I open my legs, offering myself to him. His cock is straining against the front of his pants, as he moves to lie down on his stomach. His warm breath flutters over my wetness as he growls out "Mine" just before his tongue swipes at my entrance.

Falling onto the pillow, I moan in pure ecstasy. My fingers clutch his hair, holding him against me as my eyes roll back.

"Yesss," I sigh.

He reaches his hand up under my shirt, pressing his palm flat over my stomach. He stops, forcing my eyes wide as I peer down at him ready to beg him to continue.

His lips trail a path over my mound to my thigh. I love the devious look in his eyes as he torments me. I want to grab him by his hair again, forcing him back to where I want him, but when his mouth trails a path up toward my stomach, his face turns serious.

There's so much emotion in one stare before his eyes slowly close and he leans forward, pressing a kiss against my lower belly. He pauses for a moment before looking back up at me.

"I want to put a baby here," he whispers. His voice is so low that for a second, I wonder if I dreamed it up.

Tears fill my eyes. I've thought about the day we'd have kids, but I've never let myself picture it happening out of fear of wanting it too much. I envision his face lighting up when he holds a blonde-haired little boy with blue eyes matching his own. I imagine his smile and the love in his eyes the first time he says "Dad" and his laughter when he chases him around the house.

My heart grows fuller when I think of the two of them standing in the kitchen, our little one standing next to Callum, as they make Mickey Mouse pancakes for breakfast like I used to do with my dad.

I subtly nod my head, unable to form a sentence. The images in my mind so vivid, they've stolen my words. All I've ever wanted was a family of my own.

"I want a baby with you, too."

chapter three

CALLUM
october

"Do you really think this is necessary?" Ellie asks, running her nails over the base of my neck into my hair. "Cameras inside and outside of our house. Isn't it kind of... I don't know, weird?"

I press a kiss to her shoulder before leaning back, looking her straight in the eye.

I recently asked Graham to install a security system for us. It originally started by me wanting more eyes on our home. Living out in the middle of nowhere, you often hear sounds. There were times the motion detectors would turn on the lights and it made Ellie jumpy when we'd look outside and find nothing.

I wanted her to feel safe, and I never wanted to be put in the predicament again of not knowing who was coming and going. I knew Ellie was hesitant on the idea, but we decided to have additional cameras put in near the front door and in the kitchen, overlooking the doors leading to our back patio.

"There is nothing I wouldn't do to keep you safe, Ellie. Not a damn fucking thing. After what happened," I pause, remembering the day I went to pick her up at her house and found her gone. "The fear of not knowing who you were with or if you're okay, it's not something I want to ever relive. I want you to always feel safe in our home."

Her face softens, as the glisten of tears fill her eyes.

"Baby, don't cry."

"It's hard not to, Callum." She runs her fingers under her eye, catching the tear that threatens to fall.

A rustling sound behind us alerts us we're no longer alone. "Sorry to interrupt," Graham mutters behind us. "You're all set now."

Turning, I spot Graham and Maverick standing in the doorway to our kitchen. If there's anyone who understands the fear of something happening to the woman you love, it's Graham.

There's a look of guilt on their faces as they look from Ellie and back to me.

"Graham, I know you had cameras set up at your place. Did Halle have a hard time with it or think they were weird?" Ellie asks.

Graham's jaw flexes and I know, like me, it's hard to get the thought of the woman you love being hurt out of your head.

"There's nothing weird about making yourself feel safe in your own home. After what you've been through, I think it's necessary for both of you to have that comfort again."

Ellie went through a lot this past year. The trial dredged up a lot of painful memories. Royal is now in prison for the rest of his life, but it doesn't mean I'm not going to do everything I can to give Ellie the security and the sense of peace she still deserves after all this time.

"We're gonna clean up but wanted you to know we were done. I'll show you how everything works before we leave."

Graham nods his head toward the door as his friend and co-worker, Maverick, flashes Ellie a reassuring smile. I wave them off, telling them I'll catch up with them in a few minutes before turning back to Ellie.

"See, baby, nothing weird about it."

Ellie runs her finger over her bottom lip, lost in thought. I skim my hand over her shoulder, hoping to pull her from wherever her mind has ran off to before she brings her focus back to me.

"You're right," she sighs, wrapping her arms around my waist, hugging me.

I press my mouth against the side of her head, kissing her firmly. "I'd do anything for you. You know that, right?"

"I do," she mumbles, her body trembles as the emotions she's working to contain let loose.

"Please don't cry," I whisper.

She takes a heavy breath before pulling back. "I think I'm going to go outside to read for a little bit." She reaches to grab her book off the counter, as she tucks a strand of hair behind her ear.

Some days are harder than others, but I can't push her. She's learning to move forward one day at a time.

When she gets to the patio door, she turns to look back at me, knowing I'm watching every step of the way.

"I'm okay," she says reassuringly. I don't know if it's more for me or for herself, but she gives me a small smile before pulling the door open, stepping outside, and closing it behind her. I continue to watch her as she climbs into her hammock, laying her book on her lap.

I stand here, watching her through the sliding glass door, wanting to make sure she is okay, before turning to search for Graham and Maverick, finding them in the entryway. Graham is bent down picking up boxes as Maverick messes with the tablet, adjusting the settings.

"Everything okay?" Graham finishes folding up a box, stacking it along with several others into a larger one, as he shuffles papers together.

"Yeah, I think with what happened to Halle recently and now the cameras, things are just resurfacing for her again. She'll be okay though."

"I hear ya," Graham says, as Maverick hands him the tablet. He walks me through how to check the cameras, adjusting their focus and the different views.

"I owe you for getting this all set up for us. I think this will help give her some peace of mind."

"Of course, man. If you need anything, just hit me or Maverick up. We are always here for you both."

Maverick nods his head, agreeing.

"We're getting ready to head to Brodie's for lunch, if you want to join us."

Glancing out the window in the living room to Ellie outside, I debate it for a few minutes, knowing she would want me to go even though I'd rather be here with her right now.

I nod. "Yeah." I motion to the backyard where Ellie is. "I'm gonna check on her, make sure she's good. I'll meet you there."

Maverick reaches for the door and they both throw a wave over their shoulder, as they take the empty boxes and head outside.

Cutting across the living room, I make a beeline toward the back patio. Ellie looks startled when she hears the sliding glass door open and I step out onto the deck.

"It's okay. Just me."

"Sorry, I wasn't expecting you to come out here. I don't know why I'm all jumpy all of a sudden."

I relax onto the bench seat facing Ellie, reclining back with my arm along the banister.

"That's the exact reason why I wanted to have the security system and cameras installed in the first place."

She lets out a heavy sigh, I know dreading this conversation, as she closes her book.

"I just hate feeling like I can't live a normal life. Security systems, cameras... this isn't what I had in mind when I pictured small town living."

"Baby, that's just the way the world is today. Is it really a big deal in the grand scheme of things? This is supposed to give you peace of mind, not stress you out. Why does it bother you so much?"

"Callum, up until I met you, I didn't even own a cell phone. Excuse me for not easily coming around to the idea of having cameras hanging inside my house. It's like someone's always watching me, okay? I just, I don't like it. I'm already wearing this watch. Isn't that enough?"

She points to the Apple watch I bought her. She knows the real reason why I got it was to know no matter where she went, she'd always have a way of contacting me. Call me crazy, or maybe a little overprotective, but I thought it would make both of us feel better.

When we went through the trial, details started coming out about how Royal had been following her. There were pictures of her, ones taken inside her house, that were used as evidence.

It dawns on me then why she feels like it's her privacy being invaded once again.

"The cameras are only for times when we need them, Ellie. It's not like I'm going to sit at the office and watch you at home."

She raises her eyebrow at me, not believing a word I just said.

"What?" I hold up my hands.

"You mean to tell me the thought hadn't crossed your mind?"

"The cameras are only pointing down the hallway, overlooking the entryway, and in the kitchen. If I wanted to watch you at work, I'd install a camera in our bedroom and in the shower."

I flash her a knowing smirk before raising my eyebrows suggestively.

"Oh, lord," she sighs, clutching the book in her arm as she swings her legs over the side of the hammock.

"Well, you wanted me to come clean about what I had in mind. Those would be the only times I'd be sneaking in a peek at the cameras, outside of wanting to make sure you were safe."

She walks across the deck, eliminating the distance between us, taking a seat on my lap. She wraps her arm around my neck. Running my palm up the smooth skin of her leg, I feel her tremble beneath me. I love how her body still reacts to me, even with just the smallest of touches.

"It's just the way the world is these days. It's not uncommon for people to install security systems and cameras in their homes. Think about those nights when I'm working late at the office or I'm coming home from drinks with the guys. If you're in the room watching Netflix and hear a noise, you can pick up your phone and check to see who it is."

"Can't we just get a dog?"

"Sure, but we're not getting rid of the cameras either."

She tosses her head back letting out a frustrated groan. When her eyes meet mine again, a strand of hair falls into her face. I reach over and brush it out of her eyes.

"Look at us, married and having our first disagreement. I guess this is where we compromise. Sorry, baby, this is one thing I won't budge on."

"You're really not going to let this go, are you?" she mumbles, reaching up to wrap her fingers around her compass necklace.

"Nope," I say, punctuating the end.

"Gosh, you're so stubborn."

I can't help but laugh at that comment. She's one of the most stubborn women I know. I happen to remember how hard it was just getting her to talk to me when we first met.

"Right back atcha, babe."

"Fine," she concedes. "Only under one condition."

"What's that?"

"Guess it means no more sex in the kitchen." She grins.

Damn it.

chapter four

ELLIE

I'm standing in the kitchen spreading jam on my bread when my phone vibrates on the counter beside me. I quickly grab the towel, wiping off my hands, before swiping the screen to answer the call.

"What are ya doin'?" Kinsley darts straight to the point. Perching the phone between my ear and my shoulder, I tighten the lid and put the jar back in the fridge.

"Well, at this moment I'm making myself something to eat," as I take a large bite of my PB and J sandwich. "What are you doing?" I mumble around the bread in my mouth.

Kinsley giggles. "You live a wild life, ya know that?"

"Just the way I like it."

"Well, I was wondering if you and Brea wanted to come over tonight to hang out. Halle, understandably, is still laying low after what went down at the salon. I've been wanting to see that new movie with Denzel Washington and was thinking we could drink some wine, hang out. The guys can go do whatever guys do. Whatcha think?"

Honestly, that sounds like the perfect way to spend my Friday. My stomach rolls again. Taking a deep breath, I swallow a gulp of my water and mentally tell myself I'm okay.

I've been feeling sick to my stomach the past few days, and I'm not sure if I'm coming down with something.

"It kind of depends on how I'm feeling. I've been nauseous and tired the last few days. I'm not sure if I'm coming down with something. I don't want to get you two sick."

"You're pregnant, aren't you?"

Kinsley is never one to beat around the bush. Her straight to the point question throws me off my game. It's completely unexpected.

"What?" I choke, as I take another bite. "Jesus, Kinsley. I'm eating. Where the hell did that come from?"

"Well, I mean, it's not like it's unrealistic. Your wedding was what, two months ago?"

"I'm not pregnant," I say, almost trying to convince myself. However, despite how much it throws me off, it's incredibly likely. It's not like we haven't been practicing the art of baby making.

In fact, since we've got married, I'd say we'd been practicing quite often. We're qualified professionals now. Married life certainly has its pros.

"I couldn't be pregnant, could I?"

"Well, I guess that's a question only you would know. Have you been using protection?"

Since before Callum and I started dating, I've been on birth control. Gram got me on it when I was still a teenager in high school. I used to get the worst cramps and the doctor recommended it to help with my cycle.

For as long as I remember, I've never missed a pill. I was always on top of it. Every morning I'd wake up, take a shower, and while I was standing in the bathroom, I'd take my pill just before I'd brush my teeth.

My mind flashes back to the week of the wedding. I woke up the day before from a phone call from Kinsley saying the DJ had called and had to back out of our reservation. She was panicking so I pulled myself out of bed, threw on a pair of leggings and a baseball cap, and was out the door. I was halfway down the road when I realized I hadn't even brushed my teeth, much less my hair or even remembered to take my pill.

It was the next morning when I went about my routine and was about to take my pill that it dawned on me, I had forgotten. Kicking myself for my senseless error, I took two pills that morning telling myself certainly one day wasn't going to make that big of a difference.

Could it be I was wrong?

"Oh, Kinsley," I sigh, setting my half uneaten sandwich back down on the plate. The nerves wracking through me, making it nearly impossible to eat now.

"Don't get worried, it's going to be okay. I mean, it's not like you're young and reckless. You're married, to a man who would give you the world, and the two of you would make amazing parents. Could you imagine a little Callum running around?"

The mention of Callum as a little boy with sandy blonde hair and the cutest dimples in the world, nearly melts my heart into a puddle of goo on the floor. Callum would make the best dad.

"Do you want me to get a pregnancy test and come over? Would it make you feel better now to find out?"

I check the time on the clock and it's just after eleven in the morning. Callum won't be home until well after five.

"Would you?"

There's a quiver in my voice and Kinsley must hear it, too, as she repeats again, "It's going to be okay, Ellie. I promise."

Time seems to creep by slowly as I wander around the house aimlessly waiting for her to get here. I try to busy myself with laundry and loading the dishwasher, but the entire time my mind is on the thought of me being pregnant. I picture the look on Callum's face when I tell him, remembering the night in our bed when he told me he wanted to give me a baby.

For so long, I never thought the love I have found with Callum would ever be possible. I was just getting through life, day by day. The day I met him at the bus station, it was like my entire world shifted and everything fell into place.

Every day from that point forward, I've felt like I've been subconsciously holding my breath. Sadly, every time something good happens in my life, there is always a blow to reality reminding me never to forget how quickly it can be taken away.

There's a part of me that wants to be over the moon at the thought of having a baby of my own. Then there's the very real part of me that's terrified out of the fear it could all be taken away from me. That's the exact reason why I decide to hold off on telling Callum until I know for certain I'm pregnant, no matter what this test says.

As much as I want to see the look on his face when I tell him we're having a baby, nothing would compare to the moment I would have to tell him our dreams are no longer the reality we thought. I just couldn't bear the thought of taking this from him the same way life has taken from me countless times.

There's a harsh knock on the door and for the first time in the past hour, I'm finally moving around with a sense of urgency. My feet skid across the floor from my socks, as I hurry toward the door, swinging it open to see Kinsley standing there smiling while holding the bag in the air.

"I got the goods. Let's do this!"

Leave it to Kinsley to break up the tension I was feeling before. I can't help but laugh as her eyebrows wag, before she bounces in through the door, kicking off her shoes behind her.

"Okay," she pauses, reaching in the bag and tossing it onto the back of the couch. She pops open the box, unwrapping the stick before shoving it into my hands. "You take the little cap off the end there and pee on the end of this thing."

Crinkling my nose up, I reply, "Yeah, I've seen the commercials."

Kinsley follows along behind me to the bathroom. Leaning against the wall opposite of the door, she crosses her arms over her chest and smiles at me. "I'll wait here for you."

Flashing a forced smile, I push the door shut and go through the motions of taking the test.

"You okay in there?" Kinsley's reassuring voice filters through the crack in the door.

I push the cap back on the test and set it down on the edge of the sink, before pulling the door open.

"Well?" she asks, looking at me.

"I'm not sure yet. Still waiting," I sigh, sitting down on the edge of the bathtub massaging my forehead.

"You really shouldn't be so worried. It's going to be okay."

"Is it? I don't know the first thing about being a mom, Kinsley. Not a clue. Hell, I'm still convinced I'm failing at this whole wife thing already. Ever since we've been home, all I've been doing is lying around and sleeping. This child would be screwed."

"Oh, shut it," she says, her reassuring voice gone. I stare up at her, caught off guard by the change in her tone. "You are not failing as a wife and you most certainly would not fail as a mom. You may have had a shitty example set in front of you, but I know you've told me how amazing your dad and Grams were."

Tears well up in my eyes at her words. She's right. My mom may not have been the parent I needed her to be after I lost my dad, but I still had two amazing people in my life who showed me how to treat a child with love.

The mood shifts when Kinsley picks up the test, before glancing up at me and back down to the test.

"What?" I hurry to stand, reaching for the stick.

"I can't tell if there's a line or if I'm just imagining things. Do you see it?"

There's a faint line on the test. My eyes dart between the test and to the diagram that tells you how to determine if it's positive or not.

"Oh God, what does this mean?" I cry, looking at the faint line on the pregnancy test.

"It's okay. These types of things happen. You'll just have to make an appointment with your lady doctor, and they'll do a blood test for you. At this point, that may be the only way to know for certain."

The sound of knocking at the door forces my eyes wide.

"Good lord, Ellie, calm down. It's just Brea. She called me while you were in the bathroom and wanted to stop by."

I let out a heavy sigh of relief, as guilt rolls through my stomach. I hate how panicked I am at the thought of telling Callum right now.

Brea's sweet voice echoes down the hallway as Kinsley calls out, "We're in the bathroom."

"Hey," Brea sings, popping her head over Kinsley's shoulder. "This is a weird place to hang out. What's going on?"

"Ellie might be pregnant."

Hearing Kinsley's words was like a snap to reality. I might be pregnant. I could be a mom. Could I do this? What if something ever happened to Callum? Could I do this alone by myself? What do I have to offer this child?

Thoughts of self-doubt race through my head. The voices so loud that I can't even hear Kinsley and Brea talking to me before Kinsley waves her hand in front of my face.

"C'mon, we need you to sit down. You're looking all pale. If you don't pull yourself together before Callum gets home, he's going to know something is wrong. There's nothing for you to be worried about, seriously."

Kinsley pulls me by my hand down the hallway, as Brea wraps her arm around mine. Pushing me to sit on the couch, I pull a blanket over my lap, folding my arms over the armrest and lying my head down.

"I'll call and make you an appointment. If you want, I can even go with you to Everton."

Kinsley starts pacing in the living room as she talks on the phone with the doctor's office as Brea sits down on the floor, leaning against the front of the couch.

"What's running through your head, pretty girl?"

Brea picks up on everything. If you think for a second something can get by her, you're sadly mistaken.

"I think I'm just scared." I hate admitting those words out loud to myself.

"Well, of course you are." She laughs, picking at the edge of her shorts where the denim is frayed. "I'm pretty sure that's normal and very common for first time parents. Does this have to do with what happened with, um, your mom and all of that?"

Before the trial, the last time I had seen my mom was the day I was abducted. Seeing her face when I opened the door to run away, just before I was knocked unconscious, was hard. Callum has been there for me through the nightmares and the anxiety of having to see her in court.

My mom had suspected Royal was up to something after his release when she found papers with my name and Arbor Creek noted. She testified she learned from my aunt, who was the only person who knew where I was, that I was staying in Arbor Creek, Iowa. All those years she never believed he was hurting me, but what she found when she arrived here to come to find him, was something else entirely.

We haven't spoken to each other, but she testified in court, which helped put Royal away. I've told Callum I have no intention of speaking to her ever again, whether she believes me now or not. All I care about now is moving forward.

"She has shown me in many ways how not to act as a parent, but no, this isn't about her. It's about my dad and Gram. I know what it's like to lose the people you love. The more you let people in, the more likely they will be taken away. I couldn't bear the thought of losing Callum, Brea. I can't. If I were to lose him or if something were to ever happen to this baby," I sniff, using the edge of my thumb to wipe beneath my eye. My other arm wraps protectively around my stomach, as I let out a heavy breath. "I just don't think I'd be able to survive it. I just couldn't."

"Ellie, you're the strongest person I know. What you've been through," Brea says, scooching closer to me, running her thumb under my eye catching a tear. "You deserve to have all those sad times left in the past and move onto happier times. I know you're scared, but you have so much to look forward to in your future. Don't let your fears take that away from you. You deserve to finally have your happy ending."

"Thank you," I mutter, as she kneels next to me to give me a hug.

"Of course. You're stubborn as hell sometimes, but I'll always be here to remind you that your family is bigger than you think it is. You'll never go through anything alone again."

chapter five

ELLIE

There are two knocks on the door as the doctor peeks her head inside, smiling. "Ellie?"

"Yes, hi." My nerves feel like they are shot. I wish I would've taken Kinsley up on her offer now to come with me to this appointment because I hate going through this alone.

I didn't though because for most of my life, I took care of myself. I promised myself I'd come and get the results of the test, then if it came back positive, I'd make sure Callum could come with me to every appointment from here on out.

"I'm Doctor Sattler, it's good to see you. How are you feeling?" She takes a seat, holding a clipboard in her hands as she scoots closer to me.

"I'm okay, I think. Just anxious to find out the results."

"I bet. Let's get onto them then, shall we? Do you have any kids yet?"

I shake my head as I twist my hands in my lap. I wish she'd just get on with it already.

Sensing my unease, she bypasses the twenty-one questions and looks over her clipboard once again before looking back at me.

"We did get the results of your blood test back and after looking them over, we can confirm that you are in fact pregnant. Congratulations."

I hear all my blood pumping, as the adrenaline courses through me. Immediately after hearing the results, I wish Callum were here. He's the only person who could calm me down and reassure me right now.

"We were unable to confirm the exact day of conception since you were uncertain of the first day of your last period."

"I just don't normally get one, I've been on the pill since I was about thirteen years old, so it's hard telling. I honestly didn't even think it would be possible to get pregnant this easily."

She laughs and I hate how stupid I feel saying that out loud. "It happens every day. You're not the first person to make that mistake though, it's okay. We will just do a quick ultrasound to confirm your due date. One question I do have for you, is dad in the picture?"

It's like there's a ball of guilt lodged in my throat, making it difficult to swallow. I hate how she automatically assumes I'm going to be raising this baby on my own because Callum isn't here with me.

"Yes, he is. He's just, uh, he's at work right now. I hadn't told him yet since I was still wanting to be certain. It was all unexpected, so I was going to wait. I wish I hadn't though since I know we'll be seeing the baby."

"You'll have another one around twenty weeks as well. We like to check to see how the baby is growing and this is a good time to find out the gender. No worries, there's still a chance for him to join you and see the baby before he or she is born."

Her smile is warm and reassuring, even though I wish Callum were here to enjoy this special moment with me.

I don't believe there's anything that can prepare you for the feeling of seeing your baby growing inside your stomach. The sound of his or her heart beating, filling the air around you, matching your own, beating wildly. The flutter of butterflies in my stomach as tears threaten to fall. The only thing that could've made this moment any better were if Callum were here holding my hand.

"If I had to guess, it looks like you're due around May 19th. Congratulations!" She smiles a warm smile seeing the emotion on my face, as she hands me a tissue.

"I'm so sorry." I laugh, wiping the tears away while fanning my face.

"Don't be sorry. This is supposed to be one of the happiest moments of your life. I hate to break it to you; the tears don't stop when you're pregnant either. Emotions sometimes get the best of you."

I thank her, as she hands me a strip of pictures she printed out. I stare at them in awe and wonder, as I walk out of the building and sit in my car staring at the life we created. I can't wait to share the news with Callum.

Checking the clock on the dash, I still have just shy of forty minutes before my shift at Hudson's. The drive there from Everton will take about thirty, so I decide to stop and pick up a sandwich as I hit the road.

My phone vibrates in my purse, and I press the button on my steering wheel connecting the call. Callum's deep voice filters through the speakers.

"Hey, baby." His voice hums through the line, and I can't help the smile that stretches across my face. "How'd the appointment go? Everything okay?"

"Yeah, everything is perfect. I have something to tell you tonight."

The phone gets muffled, and I hear Callum talking to someone. Even through all the commotion, I pick up on Randy's deep voice in the background before Callum is back on the line.

"Sorry about that, sweetheart. You have something to tell me? You know I'm an impatient man. You can just tell me now."

"No, I want to tell you in person. It'll be worth the wait though."

"Only if you insist. I'll call you on your break. You remembered your watch, right?"

I smile down at the watch he got me around my wrist. He knows I'm terrible about carrying a phone, it's not something I've ever liked having to do. Call me old school but having all these high-tech gadgets like my phone connected to my car stereo and my watch is not something of importance to me. After what's happened to me, I know how imperative it is to Callum that I'm able to connect with him anytime I need to.

"Of course, I did," I reassure him.

"Alright, baby, I'll talk to you later. Have a good day and remember I love you."

I don't know what I'd do without him here, looking out for me, wanting to take care of me. "Love you, too, handsome."

I picture him leaning back in his office chair, his sexy smirk lining the curve of his mouth. His facial hair longer, just how I like it. He was standing in the bathroom this morning getting ready to shave, and I begged him to leave it. I love it when he grows it out a little and how it feels against my palm when I run my hand over the side of his face.

Pulling up to Hudson's Grocery a little while later, I pull into a parking spot near the back of the lot and shove my keys into my back pocket. I'm so anxious to tell someone the news, but I want the first person I tell to be Callum. He deserves to share this moment with me.

The bell dings as I enter the store, and I hear Hudson's sweet voice greet me. "Morning, Ellie."

"Morning," I sing, bounding over to him to say hello with a kiss on the cheek.

Hudson is more of the grandfather I never had. As Kinsley's biological grandpa, I think it's what's bonded me to her. They both have this undying need to help people.

When Callum and I were planning our wedding, I debated back and forth on whether I was going to walk down the aisle alone or not. My father passed away when I was nine and the thought of anyone but him walking with me was hard to accept.

On the other hand, if it weren't for Hudson, I don't believe I'd be where I am today. I still remember when I called him from the pay phone asking about the ad I saw for the house for rent in Arbor Creek. He could pick up on my hesitancy to move away.

Hudson offered me more than a place to live. He gave me this job. He took me in, he looked out for me, and watched over me. There were many nights I would lie awake in bed and pray to my dad he'd get me out of Garwood. I believe he brought Callum and Hudson into my life for a reason and despite wishing it were my dad who walked me down the aisle, giving me away, I know he'd be happy I had Hudson step in for him on my big day.

I walk back to the break room and drop off my keys and jacket before punching in and heading back to the front of the store.

"You have it from here?" Hudson asks, as he finishes stacking candy before breaking down the box. "I promised June I'd meet her for lunch, and I need to make a run to the bank. I won't be gone more than an hour."

I wave him off, reassuring him I have it from here as I take over stocking the shelves with more Halloween candy.

A short while later, after I've finished sorting the goodies, I head back toward the front of the store and do more organizing. A group of kids came in earlier looking to spend their allowance on candy, tearing through the aisle and leaving it in a disarray.

The sound of a voice clearing from behind startles me.

"Hello." The ominous voice acknowledges me.

"Hi there, you ready to checkout?"

"Yes."

Tossing the candy onto the shelf, I turn to smile at the gentleman behind me. Expecting to find another friendly face from Arbor Creek, I have to force a smile on my face when I find the opposite.

His dark hair is longer, tucked behind the back of his ears, with his red trucker cap pulled down covering most of his face. That's not what sends off alarm bells in my mind. No, it's the stench of alcohol on his breath hitting me from the moment I turn around, mixed with the strong aroma of cigarette smoke.

Forcing myself to breathe, I paste a smile on my face while mentally telling myself to get through it. Help this man purchase his items and send him on his way.

Everything in me wants to fall to the ground and curl into a ball, but I don't. I've come so far in the past few months. I have fought hard to move on from the torment of my past following me. It's not just me anymore. I have so much more to live for now, and I'm not going to let my PTSD cripple me any longer.

I can do this. I know I can do this.

My fingers quickly type in my employee number on the old register, as he sets the case of beer down on the counter. I quickly slide it over the scanner, ringing it up.

"Will that be all for you, sir?"

For the first time since turning around, I look up and make eye contact with him. It's like a snap of the fingers, and I'm back in the dirty old basement of the abandoned house.

"I think you know what I want," he slurs.

Struggling to swallow, my vision gets hazy as my heart rate picks up in speed.

"I'm sorry?" I ask, not understanding what he means.

Tingles spread out across my skin, as I suddenly feel dizzy. I concentrate on the words my therapist went over with me.

Focus on your happy place.

Breathe in.

Picture sitting by the pond in your backyard with Callum.

Now breathe out, Ellie.

"Empty the register," he commands, jostling me from my thoughts.

"I don't, I - I - I don't have any money in here. We just did a shift change. The register was emptied, and the deposit was taken to the bank."

"I don't fucking believe you for a second. Listen here, bitch. I want you to call up Hudson and tell him you need him to get back here. I know he keeps a safe in the back. I want you to call him, tell him you need some help. I want him to empty that safe and you're going to help me do it."

"O-O-Okay," I stutter.

Bending down, I reach for the phone we keep beneath the counter.

"The fuck you think you're doing?" he shouts. "You put your hands in the fucking air where I can see 'em or you'll be eating this."

He raises a knife in the air, pressing the blade against the column of my neck. Just like that, once again, one man threatens to hurt me, taking everything I've ever wanted right along with him.

 chapter six

ELLIE

Keeping my hands up in front of me, I see Callum's name on my watch as the phone begins to ring. The vibration in my back pocket gives it away immediately, as his eyes dart to me.

"What's that noise?"

"It's my phone. It's my husband," I pause, not sure where to go with it. "He always calls me on my break. If I don't answer, he'll wonder if something is wrong."

"NO!" he shouts, cutting me off. His eyes turn frantic.

"Okay, okay." My voice breaks as the panic starts to rise up my throat. "I won't answer it. I just know if I don't, he'll start to wonder if something is wrong and drop by here. He worries a lot about me, he's kind of overprotective."

The words "kind of" are loose in this situation. Callum is a lot worried where I'm concerned. After what happened to me with Royal, if he had it his way, I wouldn't leave his side. That's extreme though, he knows it, and I know it. We've talked to a therapist a lot about how we have both coped with our fears that still torment us today.

Callum holds a lot of guilt over not being there to protect me. If he had any idea the situation I was in, I know without a shadow of a doubt he'd be coming in guns blazing to get me out of harm's way. It's just the way he is. Life has changed us, but I love him for always wanting to take care of me. I wouldn't change that about him whatsoever.

My phone vibrates again and, once again, as Callum's name flashes on the screen.

"He's just going to keep calling," I say calmly. "I can turn it on speaker phone. I'll tell him I'm having lunch with a friend. He won't think anything of it, I swear. I just don't want him to worry."

His face looks maniacal, darting from me to the front door of the store before falling back on mine.

"Yeah, yeah..." He hesitates. "Make it quick. Don't try to pull anything or I swear to fucking God, it will be the last time you'll ever talk to him again."

He raises the knife back up to me, forcing my heart to hammer in my chest as I nod my head frantically.

"Okay, it's okay. Please just don't point that at me. I can't be calm on the phone with him if you do and if I'm scared, he'll hear it in my voice."

He clutches the knife into his fist, leaning against the edge of the counter, before nodding his head toward me to answer it.

Pulling my phone out of my pocket, I swipe the screen answering the call and put it on speaker.

"Hey, baby," I greet him.

"Hi sweetheart." Callum's voice filters through the phone. Just hearing his voice, I feel the smile on his face, wrapping around me like a warm hug. It's almost startling how calm I am compared to the way I felt just a moment ago. "How's work going?"

"Okay," I say, looking up at the man. His jaw locks, his eyes widening as he nods to me, not liking my response. He wants me to speed it along, so I do as he wishes.

"I have you on speaker. I'm just eating a sandwich, sitting here in the break room. You'll never guess who stopped by to see me."

"Who's that, baby?" I know he's expecting me to answer with one of my girlfriends' names.

"Royal," I say, pausing to make sure he heard me. He goes silent, and I know he's probably holding the phone against his ear, praying he hadn't heard me correctly.

"Are you, are you there?" I ask, my voice growing shaky. I force myself to stay calm. If I let on that I'm nervous or scared, I'm afraid the man will pick up on the clue I've given Callum.

"You said Royal?"

"Yeah, he stopped by to bring me lunch. Isn't that sweet of him?"

There's a sound of a chair screeching in the background. I imagine the terrified look on Callum's face, but he doesn't say anything. He knows something's not right, and I'm grateful he knows me well enough to pick up on my warning for help.

"That's very sweet of him," Callum says. His sweet voice earlier has gone cold. There's fear laced with a threat in his tone now.

"Is Hudson there?"

"No, he is with June."

The man moves his hand, urging me to end the phone call. In doing so, he adjusts his knife pointing it at me as his eyes grow wide in warning.

"I gotta go," I say matter-of-factly. "Um, I'll call you when I get off work. Callum, I love you."

The emotion and the fear of it being the last time I could ever say those words to him are like a ball of cotton lodged in my throat.

"I love you, too, baby. I'll see you soon."

He reaches forward, snapping the phone out of my hand pressing the end button and tosses it behind him, sending it crashing to the ground, sliding across the floor.

"Don't get too ahead of yourself there, sweetness. I don't think that will be happening anytime soon. Put your hands back up in the air."

Bile rises in my throat, as I force my spine steel straight. I want to let the fear take over, pinning me down and holding me in place, but I don't. I won't submit to his intimidation. I've lived my whole life falling victim to the terrible things that've happened to me. I refuse to let someone come in here and threaten to take away the two things I love more than anything in this world. It'll be a cold day in hell before I let that happen.

"I'm not doing anything, I swear." I gulp, feeling a lump in my throat.

My watch flashes and I'm grateful my hands are still up in the air as a text message from Callum reading, "911" flashes on my screen. It's the same message I sent to him the day Royal had taken me. Relief washes through me, knowing he picked up on my warning. He's trying to tell me help is on the way.

Now all I have to do is just bide my time and stay calm, as the time slowly ticks.

"How much longer until Hudson should be back?"

"He normally takes short lunches, so it shouldn't be too much longer."

He starts to pace, walking up toward the front of the store, before pacing back to me. Stopping to glance out the window, he looks back to me before he resumes the same pace in front of the register counter.

My arms have started to slouch from the pain of keeping them raised in the air.

"Keep your hands where I can see them. I'm not playing games with you."

When he shifts to move, I catch for the first time the gun tucked into the back of his jeans.

I force myself to swallow. I'm scared if Hudson comes back here, something could happen to him. I don't want to see anyone I love get hurt again.

"I will be honest with you. Hudson told me he was going to the bank during his break. I don't know how much money he's gonna have here."

The loud smack ricochets around the room, as he uses his closed fist around the knife to hit me. Pain radiates through my jaw, feeling like it was split in two. My ears ring as tears fill my eyes, threatening to fall. I press my palm against my cheek.

"I don't need your advice. I've got it from here. Quit talking!"

His eyes look wild, as sweat trickles down his face. He swipes it using the back of his hand, using his fist clutching the knife to cover his mouth while contemplating something.

I just hope and pray whatever he is thinking, he's going to take it easy on me. Whatever it is he needs, I know if there is a way of me making it out of here alive and unharmed, I will have to appeal to what he wants. It's clear he's willing to go to extreme risks to get whatever money he needs.

"You can take anything you want, anything. I'll give you all the money in the register, but please, just don't hurt me."

My voice trembles, fear and adrenaline taking over me.

"You really don't know how to fuckin' listen, do ya? You just keep that pretty little mouth shut before I find something to put in it."

This all starts to feel like a bad dream. One I've relived every night I lay my head down and close my eyes. As every second ticks away, I just hold onto hope it's one second closer to when Callum is in my arms again.

The tears that once filled my eyes now seep out of the corners. I'm realizing no matter how far I've run, how hard I've fought, I'm always going to be scarred by my past.

chapter seven

CALLUM

The adrenaline coursing through me right now is the only thing fueling my body to move. The thought of what Ellie experienced the last time she was in danger urges me to move as quickly as I can to get to her.

Anyone who doesn't know Ellie's story would think Royal was just a friend of ours. Only the people closest to her would know it's the name of the sick, vile scum of the earth who put his hands on her when she was still a child. The man who broke her down and hurt her in ways no person should ever have to experience, especially by someone you're supposed to be able to trust.

The only thing protecting that sick son of a bitch now is the fact he's behind bars for the rest of his life. If he were to see freedom outside of that steel cell he's currently spending his life in, I'd be the one to see to it he's put where he truly belongs, and that's burning in hell for eternity.

Unlike the last time, I know how to find her. My hands shake as I log into my computer and pull up her Apple iCloud account. As soon as she mentioned having lunch with Royal, I needed to know if she was still at work like she should've been. What if she didn't make it to work? What if something happened on the way?

Once the GPS loaded on my screen, I nearly flipped the chair backward, shoving it away from the desk against the wall. Randy, my stepfather, knew something was up when I shouted at him to call the police and send them to Hudson's Grocery. Whoever she's with is not someone she felt safe with, and I won't feel right until she's in my arms again.

I'm grateful my office at Whitt Construction is not far from where Ellie works. Tearing out of the parking lot and down the road, I quickly dial Hudson's number. My stomach twists when he answers the call with a simple "Callum" in his jolly voice. It's clear he has no idea what's happening at the store, so I try to be quick and calm as I fill him in on my conversation with Ellie.

"She said she was with Royal?" he asks. The fear and trepidation in his voice matches my own.

"That's what she said. Do you know if anyone was there with her before you left?"

"No, we were slow today. It was just the two of us, but I left about thirty minutes ago to have lunch with June. I was going to stop by the bank to make a deposit on my way back to the store."

Pulling into the back of the parking lot of Hudson's, I breathe a small sigh of relief when I spot Ellie's car parked in the back of the lot.

"I'm here now. Do me a favor and stay away. I have the cops on their way, but they're coming from Everton, so it could still be a few minutes. The door in the back of the store, any chance you'd leave it unlocked?"

"Not normally, but I was unloading boxes from a shipment we got in earlier this morning. It should still be unlocked."

"Thanks," I say, cutting off the conversation and ending the call. I don't have time to chat. I only have one focus on my mind and that is getting to Ellie.

Grabbing the gun from the holster where it sits in my center console, I check to make sure it's loaded before jumping out of the truck and sliding it in the back of my jeans. Jogging across the lot toward the loading dock, I'm cautious to avoid making too much noise.

The sound of a buzzer goes off, and I hurry to grab the handle to pull the door closed behind me.

"Motherfucker," I whisper to myself, frantically looking around to make sure no one might have heard me.

I've never been in the back of the store before, but I opt to cut across to the other side. If Hudson is on lunch, I know it's not possible she's on her break too. I quickly check the rooms in the back for any sign of Ellie. When I find the break room in the back corner, I quickly flip on the light and see Ellie's purse hanging from the wall before turning the light back off.

I decide to come around from the back of the store, knowing if she is with someone, the element of surprise will be in my favor if I approach from behind. Pulling the gun from my waistband, I reach up and wipe the sweat from my brow with the sleeve of my shirt.

The closer I get, the more I make out the sound of his voice. What I hear next makes the blood in my veins run cold.

"You can take anything you want, anything. I'll give you all the money in the register, but please, just don't hurt me." Her voice comes out a whimper. The sound makes me want to run to her and wrap her in my arms.

Hearing him threaten to hurt her flips a switch inside me, one that I've worked to contain for so long after Ellie was hurt.

Keeping the gun pressed against my side, I look over the aisle and see a man pacing back and forth in front of the counter where the register sits. He takes a step forward and Ellie's beautiful and heartbroken face comes into my view and the ache in my chest lessens.

Her face is red, tears streaming, as she's struggling to contain her emotions. There's a bruise forming on her face. The anger coiling in me tightens like a knot deep in my gut. Her arms are raised in the air, but the way her shoulders sag, I know the pain of holding her hands up is weighing on her.

His pacing continues. By the look of his jerky movements and unsure footing, he's been drinking. If I had to guess, he's probably had one too many which works in my favor.

When he stops in front of Ellie again, pointing the knife in her face, he demands she stop crying. He runs a hand through his hair before adjusting his hat, muttering to himself, but his words are hard to make out.

"You're gonna have to come with me," he finally says. My eyes are wide with fear. I can't let her leave with him.

Thinking about where he could take her, what could happen to her, I won't let it happen.

"Wh-why?" Ellie stammers. "Where are you going to take me?"

"I told you to stop asking fucking questions. If you keep this shit up…" he says, pointing the tip of the knife toward Ellie. Her face trembles, and that's it for me.

"Put your fucking knife down!" I yell, taking him off guard. I have him right where I want him. His back is to me, but he's facing Ellie.

The only thing working in my favor is knowing the counter is separating him from her. One rash movement and I'll take him down without a single hesitation.

"Who the fuck is this?" he questions, his head snapping back to me over his shoulder before looking back at Ellie.

"Quit asking questions," I retort, throwing his earlier threats back to him. "It's my turn to ask questions, but first, put the knife down. If you hurt my wife, so help me God I will live out the rest of my days making yours miserable. Do you fucking hear me?"

His head darts back to Ellie, before bouncing back to mine. It must be the mention of her being my wife that throws him off.

"You really are the crazy bastard she says you are." He laughs. "She said you'd show up here like this. I'm glad she finally told you about me."

"I'm sorry?" I question.

"It's terrible you had to learn about us this way."

Ellie's eyes are wide with horror at his insinuation, flashing over to mine. Her arms waiver, silently telling me it's not true. He's gotta be out of his motherfucking mind if he thinks I'd ever think she'd choose this piece of shit over me.

"So, you're the Royal she's been telling me about, huh?" I bait him.

"Oh, so she has mentioned me then?" He laughs again, this time sounding more like a cackle. It's sinister and disturbing, and it's then I realize I don't want to drag this out anymore. This fucker likely doesn't know the history and who Royal truly is, but I'll make him pay for it just the same.

When he turns his head back to look at Ellie, her eyes flash to me. When they do, I nod my head to her telling her to move out of the way.

Her throat bobs as she takes a forceful swallow. The fear and panic are evident on her face at the thought of what could happen next. The cops are going to be here any minute, and I'm afraid once he realizes his plan has failed, he'll get angry.

"She's mentioned you alright. Did she give you my message by chance?" I ask, as he turns back to look at me. In that same movement, Ellie rushes out of the way and I dive toward him, as we both stumble against the counter.

Despite being unsteady on his feet, his grip on the knife doesn't waiver. Wrapping my arm around his, I attempt to control his lower arm to the floor. Ellie's cries from behind us begs us to stop, but I drown them out focusing on his face.

"I guess she didn't tell you how I said if I ever saw your face as a free man, I'd be sure to send you straight back to hell where you belong."

I can almost picture I'm staring at Royal. My anger intensifies nearly throwing me off, letting up on the grip I have on his arm. An evil smile spreads wide on his face, realizing my mistake, as he takes the knife in his hand, driving it up into the side of my stomach.

"No!" Ellie screams.

My body hunches over trying to protect myself, as the knife twists before he pushes me backward, sending me crashing to the floor.

The taste of blood fills my mouth. The last thing I remember before the darkness pulls me under is the sound of the loud commands in the background from police and Ellie's sad face, full of pain and heartbreak as she mutters the words, "Please, Callum, don't leave me. Oh, God, please don't take him, too."

chapter eight

ELLIE

The sound of police shouting out orders and sirens blaring replay over and over in my head. Clutching my arms around my stomach, I press my back against the wall of the hospital, sliding down to curl into a ball.

I hate everything about being in this hospital. The last time we were here resurfaces so many terrible memories and, once again, I'm faced with the cruelty of the world and the uncertainty of whether I'll ever get to see Callum's face again.

Why does it feel like every time things are starting to look up for me, life wants to come crashing in and remind me it's not as good as it seems?

Tears fall from my eyes in waves. I don't know how long I sit here, cold and crying, when the sound of Brea's soft voice pulls me from my turmoil.

"Oh, God, Ellie. It's going to be okay," she whispers, wrapping her warm arms around me. She hugs me, holding me as we both cry together on the hallway floor before Mason's soothing voice pulls us both up to stand. He drapes his jacket over me. Only then do I realize the blood staining my shirt and my hands.

"No, no, no," I cry, shaking as I hold my hands out in front of me. Mason covers me in his coat, ushering me down the hall.

"It's okay, Ellie. He's going to fight through this. I promise you, he's gonna fight for you. Let's get you cleaned up."

With Brea's arms around me and the jacket draped over my shoulders, I pull the coat tighter, hoping to block off the blood I can't get out of my mind.

Mason tells us to stand right here, as he jogs over to the nurses' station a few feet away. He mutters something to the nurse, her wide eyes darting to me before nodding. He runs his hand over his jaw and, in that moment, when he thinks I'm not looking, I see the pain and fear on his face. The thought of losing his older brother starts to set in, and the knot in my stomach tightens at the possibility of losing Callum.

My hands wrap around my stomach, picturing the life growing inside me, raising this little boy or little girl without their father. I know what it's like to lose your parent. The finality of death taking everything away. My heart aches thinking how Callum may never know he is going to be a dad, sending another wave of emotion crashing through me.

"Oh, Ells," Brea murmurs, hugging me again.

"I never got the chance to tell him," I mumble against her shoulder. I can barely get the words out and my chest hurts hearing those very words spoken aloud. "I went to the doctor today and confirmed everything. I never got to, he doesn't know."

I pull back, staring Brea in the eyes, seeing the dread and sadness she's trying to keep hidden, trying to stay strong for me. But we don't know what's going on, if he's going to be okay. I can't expect her to have the answers for me, but right now I wish she'd just lie to me and pretend like she does.

"Come here, let's get you cleaned up," Mason says, ushering us to follow behind the nurse who leads us into a private room.

I'm in a daze as Mason helps me to the sink, turning on the water and squirting soap into my hands. Brea uses a towel and water to wipe blood I didn't even know was on my chest and cheek from when I held Callum when he laid there lifeless on the floor.

I hear the nurses' muffled words behind us, how she has brought me a change of clothes until I am able to get something else to wear. She sets them on the chair next to us.

"Do you want me to stay in here with you while you change?" Brea asks, handing me a towel to dry my hands off. It takes me a second to comprehend her words as I slowly shake my head.

"I can do it. You don't have to help me but thank you."

"I know I don't have to, Ellie. I'm here if you need me though."

I nod, as her and Mason move to the door. Brea looks back at me once, giving me another chance before she follows him out into the hallway.

Standing in front of the mirror on the wall, I stare at the blood staining my shirt as tears form in my eyes. I bite down on my lip, trying to stop it from quivering, as I reach for the hem of my shirt and pull it over my head.

My hand trembles as I run my palm over my stomach. The thought of raising this baby without Callum sends another wave of emotions tidaling through me. It's like the waters are coming at me from all directions, pulling me under, and I can't breathe.

The only things keeping me holding on by a thread are this baby and the hope that Callum will make it through surgery. He was so strong for me when it was me in this position. Knowing now the fear he had felt waiting for the police to give him news, for me to wake up, I understand how hard this was on him.

He didn't give up though. He prayed and prayed for me to fight. I've been through far too much to give up and let someone threaten to take away everything I've ever wanted.

When you're standing with all you've ever wanted before you and the threat of someone taking that away, are you just going to throw in the towel and walk away? No. You fight because anything worth having is worth fighting over.

Promise me you will no longer be held back by your fears and you'll follow your dreams.

Reaching up, I clasp my hand around my compass necklace, the gift from my grams. I draw strength from the woman who gave me so much when it felt like everything was drained out of me. When I felt like all my strength was gone and the will to fight had been ripped away, she reminded me of the happiness both her and my father would've wanted for me.

Leaning forward, I grab the scrub top left for me on the chair and pull it over my head. I run my fingers under my eyes, wiping away the streaks of mascara left on my face and let out a heavy sigh.

"It's gonna be okay. He's going to be okay. Just breathe, Ellie. Remember to just breathe."

I nod my head, mentally reminding myself of my mantra to just breathe, as I head back out to the hallway to be with my friends until we hear more.

Opening the door, the first person I see is Kinsley as she rushes toward me wrapping her arms around me.

"Oh my God," she cries.

I hug her back, but the tears from earlier don't fall. I almost feel numb.

"You promised me you wouldn't scare me like this again." She leans back, reaching up to swipe the tear under her eye away before stepping away. Her hand finds mine, squeezing as she flashes me a forced smile.

"I'm sorry," I reply, remembering the comment she made the day in the hospital moments after I woke up.

"I'm looking for the family of Callum Reid," the commanding voice cuts in through the waiting room just as I glance over and see Callum's mom, Connie, push through the doors toward me.

Her eyes are red with anguish, as Randy follows along behind her.

I raise my hand up to the doctor. "That's us," as Connie rushes over. I recognize him as the same doctor who helped treat me when I was in the hospital, and it's like a twisted form of déjà vu.

"Hello," he says, his eyes narrowing as if he's trying to recall where he may know me from. He doesn't press it, and I'm thankful because I'd rather focus on what he's about to tell us and not relive the past anymore than I already do.

"I'm Doctor Kline. Callum sustained a stab wound to his abdomen. While he lost a lot of blood, we were able to give him a transfusion. The good news is it just barely missed his liver. Had the wound been any higher, he would've lost a lot more blood and it's hard telling where he would be."

Oh, God.

"So, what does that mean? Will he be okay?"

No offense but get to the damn point.

He nods his head. "We had to do some repairs to his intestines, so he'll be sore for some time, but he should be okay."

Hearing him say those words, *"he should be okay,"* gives me a renewed hope.

He's going to be okay. Reaching up to rub my hand over my stomach, I tell myself for the second time we're going to be okay.

chapter nine

CALLUM

The sound of the door clicking as it shuts startles me awake. Turning my head, I find Ellie curled up asleep in the chair next to my hospital bed. She hasn't left my side since I got out of surgery, and I'm relieved to see she's finally able to rest.

"You scared the crap out of her, ya know? Out of all of us. She was terrified by the amount of blood you had lost that you were never going to make it out of surgery," Brea says, as she leans back against the wall next to my brother, Mason.

Halle and Graham are with them, taking a seat on the couch on the other side of the room. They've been through their share of shit recently, so I know they understand the reality of how badly this could've turned out.

I nod. "I'm okay though," I say, just as my brother glances up to look at me. He looks tired, but he's being strong.

Ellie stirs, blinking her eyes awake as she sits up, reaching over to grab my hand. I smile when I see her sleepy face, as a small smile curves her mouth.

"How you feeling?"

"Better now," I sigh, as a sharp pain stings my side taking my breath away.

"Are you sure? What's wrong?" Ellie says, standing to check me over.

"Nothing, it's just sore, baby. I promise, you don't have to worry."

I rub my thumb over the back of her hand, and I feel her relax some. There's a comfort having all of our friends here with us. Ellie, Brea, and Halle talk about the news of Brea's friend, Lissa, who recently moved to Arbor Creek. We all know there's something going on between her and Brannon, especially after our trip to Chicago for our joint bachelor and bachelorette party, even though they are both too stubborn to admit it to anyone else.

Mason, Graham, and I talk about the Iowa football game. Graham and Mason are both animated as they recount the end of the game where Iowa came back, scoring at the last minute to beat Wisconsin.

When the nurse stops in later to check in and give me more pain medicine, they excuse themselves to head home for the night, reassuring us they'll be by to check in with us over the next couple of days. Ellie hugs both Brea and Halle goodbye, whispering quietly to them, as they rub her arm reassuringly before they disappear out the door.

Ellie climbs back into her chair next to me, reaching out once again to hold my hand.

"You sleep okay earlier, sweetheart?"

"Not as good as I would if I had you next to me," she replies, lacing her fingers in mine before running her fingers over my palm. She is lost in thought, and I suspect the fear of her losing me is back on her mind.

"You can climb up here, baby," I mutter, trying to scoot over enough to make room for her next to me.

Ellie hesitates for a second, but her need to be next to me wins out. She stands and carefully climbs on the bed. Her head rests on my shoulder as she wraps her arm over my lower stomach, deliberately avoiding the bandages covering my side.

She smells like flowers, and that, combined with her warmth pressed against me, washes over me, cleansing me from the hallow and sterile walls surrounding us.

I sigh, leaning into her touch. "I can't wait until we're home."

"Me either." I sense there's more she wants to say.

"How are you doing with everything?"

The silence surrounds us as she thinks about how to respond. It feels like several minutes pass before she finally replies, but it was probably no more than just a few seconds. The time weighs heavily on me, realizing how hard this has been on her.

"I'm better now that I know you're going to be alright."

"It's going to take a lot more than some lunatic to take me away from you, Ellie."

"I know you'd fight for me, for us. I just couldn't bear the thought of losing you. I've lost so many people in my life, Callum. So many people."

There's a break in her voice, the emotions getting caught in her throat. I hate thinking about what she could be feeling right now.

"I've been thinking lately about how much I wish you could've met my dad and Grams. They would've loved you. It was hard to think about how they weren't there for our wedding, but it's times like this I wish they were still here to help me through. I couldn't imagine if I lost you, what I would do."

"You don't need to fear losing me, baby. As long as I'm still breathing, I'm fighting every day for you. For us."

"Just having you by my side gives me strength. I can do anything, as long as I have you. I think someday I'll actually be able to move on from the past, especially when I think about all we have to look forward to in the future."

"There's nothing we can't get through together," I say, with every ounce of conviction in me. Ellie leans her head back and I tilt mine toward her, pressing a soft kiss against her lips. She reaches her hand up, running her fingers through my hair at the base of my neck, deepening our connection.

I wish we were back at home, in our own bed, fully healed. I want to kiss her the way she deserves to be kissed. Full of every ounce of passion and love I have for her.

She pulls back, breaking our kiss as she inhales deeply. Her chest rises and falls with every breath she tries to take, and I smile to myself, loving how her body responds to me. Even lying together in a hospital bed, her body knows my touch.

She rests her head back on my shoulder. After a few minutes, I hear her breath even out as the exhaustion pulls her under. Lacing her fingers with mine, I let the sound of her soft snores and the warmth of her body envelop me, soothing me into a deep sleep.

ELLIE

It was a rough few days, but Callum was finally released from the hospital and able to come home. When we first got home, I was focused on making sure he was resting and recovering. Waking up yesterday, I felt a tremendous amount of guilt I hadn't yet told him about the baby. It felt like I was carrying a secret around, when in all honesty, I just didn't know how to tell him.

Callum has given me so much. He's always been so thoughtful in the way he's surprised me. I wanted it to be something romantic, untainted by the painful memories of the hurt we've both lived through at the hands of monsters. I hoped it would be something we could look back on and think of the life we're building and the love we have between us.

Pacing back and forth in front of the door, I hear two light knocks. Quickly looking back and forth, I look for any sign Callum could be here before looking up at the security camera.

I squint my eyes at them, hating how I'm trying to surprise him, but the eagle eyes from above are watching me like a hawk. I understand now more than ever how important it is, but I've never been a fan of technology. I wish I didn't need these to feel safe in my own home.

Opening the door, I'm greeted with Kinsley's face beaming a smile at me.

She holds the large frame covered by a bag up in the air and wags her eyebrows at me. "I got the goods!"

"Okay, come in, but hurry. Callum is in our bedroom lying down and if he hears you, I'm worried he'll check the cameras from the iPad and the surprise will be ruined."

"Alright, well, quit talking and let me in already."

I roll my eyes at her and smile, opening the door.

"Oh, God, I can't wait to hear about his reaction. If only I could be a fly on the wall when you tell him." She bounces around all giddy as she whispers to me.

"Come here, I want to get away from that dang camera," I mutter, leading her into the living room area with the bag in my hand.

Setting it on the couch, she helps me open the bag. Kinsley has been a lifesaver helping me organize this surprise for Callum. As soon as I read the quote on the frame, tears fill my eyes.

"Do you think he'll like it?"

"Are you kidding?" She laughs lightly. "Of course, he's going to like it. He's going to love it."

"I mean, the way I'm surprising him. I wanted to do something bigger, but with every day that's passed, and he doesn't know, I feel terrible I've kept it from him. Now I just want him to know."

"Ellie, the man proposed to you in the kitchen because he knew it would make it special to you. He's going to love however you choose to tell him for the simple fact it's you and it's your baby, together. I promise you, you don't need to overthink it. This is perfect."

She helps me with hanging it on the wall. I had Mason help with the measurements and making sure it was ready, we just had to get it situated for him to see it.

"Call me later and tell me all about it." She smiles, wrapping her arms around my shoulder. "I'm so damn happy for you both." Her words come out muffled against the side of my head, and I swear for a minute it sounds like she's crying.

We both freeze for a moment when we hear Callum say my name from our bedroom, as she unwraps her arms from around me. Walking backward down the hall, she waves to me and motions with her hand to call her.

I nod my head, as I scurry over to peek my head in the bedroom to check on Callum. Just as I do, I hear the front door click as Kinsley shuts it behind her.

"Hey, sweetheart, what are you doing?"

"Oh, nothing. I was just wrapping up a little something. Would you mind coming out here for a minute and giving me your opinion on it?"

His eyebrows furrow at me, uncertain of what it could be. It's not like me to keep something from him, even if it's a project I'm working on. Hell, we both know over the summer I was working on Pinterest projects left and right. It was Kinsley's doing though. She kept looking at do-it-yourself ideas for wedding decor. I still find glitter around the house from the centerpieces we made.

Wedding planning was up her alley. I would've been just as happy if we went down to the courthouse with our friends and family. After all, I just wanted to be Callum's wife. Everything else was just a bonus for me.

Pushing the door open, I walk a few feet down the hallway and wait for Callum. He's not wearing a shirt and has bandages wrapped around his torso, all taped up.

He winces and he must see the worry on my face, as he quickly smiles, reassuring me he's okay.

"What did you want to show me, babe?"

Staring over to the picture frame, I look back over at Callum. "Does this look straight to you? I just hung it up and want to make sure you're happy with it."

He looks at the large photo collage Kinsley helped me have made at this local antique store in Everton. They do a lot of crafts. When I saw the quote, "All because two people fell in love," I knew it was perfect.

It takes a minute for Callum to see what he's looking at, his eyes first scanning the photo taken of us together the night at Brodie's. It was the first night we spent together in Arbor Creek, three months after we first met. The one next to it was taken by Kinsley, without us knowing, from our first night at Wes's house for the end of summer bonfire. The next photo is of the two of us on our wedding day.

"I love that picture of us." He grins, pulling me closer to him. He presses a kiss against my lips before looking back at the other photos.

I know the moment he realizes what he's looking at when his body goes rail straight against me.

"Ellie," Callum says, a mix of awe and uncertainty lacing his voice. "Is this—what is this?"

He drops his arm from around me and takes a step forward, looking at the sonogram photo from the hospital.

"Surprise." I smile, as tears fill my eyes. His eyes bounce between me to my stomach and back up to me again, as if he's unsure what I am saying and he's afraid his hopes could be wrong.

When he sees me run my hand over my stomach, his eyes light up like I just gave him the best gift he's ever received. It makes me fall in love with him all over again.

"I'm going to be a dad?" The word "dad" comes out with more of an awe, like he doesn't know if he wants to believe it until he hears me say it out loud, not wanting to misunderstand the surprise.

"You're going to be a dad."

It's as if those six words give him permission and the dam gates were lifted, forcing a rush of emotions to come crashing through.

As if all the pain he was once feeling is gone, he drops to his knees in front of me and presses his hands against my stomach. I hear sobs racking through his body, as he quietly mumbles, "I could've lost you both."

My heart aches for him, at the thought and the picture he just painted before us. I didn't want the news to be ruined with the "what could've beens," so I quickly push it aside and try to ease his mind.

"You didn't though. We're here, we're okay. You're going to be a dad, Callum."

With both of his hands framing my stomach, he leans forward and presses his forehead softly against my non-existent bump. I have stood in front of the mirror for the past week, checking from multiple angles, hoping I would start to see the defined curve, but it hasn't come yet.

When he leans forward and presses a kiss against my stomach, I struggle to keep my emotions in check.

"I can't wait to meet you," he whispers. "I love you so much already."

There's no holding back now. The tears I was barely containing stream down my face.

"Thank you for making me the happiest man in the world."

Running my hands through his hair, I hold his head to me as he leans back to look up at me. We've been through so much together, more than I ever thought possible.

He pulls my shirt up, kissing me again on my bare stomach. His hands rub over me, over my hips, and down to my thighs. What was once a soft caress, soon turns urgent with need as Callum roughly runs his hands over my thighs and around to grab my waist.

Not caring where we are, I let him pull me down on the floor until I'm straddling him in the middle of our hallway.

He continues to push my shirt up and I help him, roughly pulling it over my head and tossing it to the side. We're both careful of his injury and where the bandage is wrapped around his side.

"I need you so bad right now," he groans, as I grind down on him. We quickly shed our pants; I help Callum with his. Positioning myself above him, I stare down at him from where he lies, his arms positioned beneath his head.

When I slowly ease down over him, I watch as his eyes slowly roll back closing them as he mutters out a low "fuck."

"Callum," I whimper. "Look at me."

His eyes flash open, blazing as he stares back at me.

"Tell me you love me."

He moves his hands up, over the top of my thighs lacing his fingers with mine.

"I love you," he mutters. "So fucking much."

In this moment, my heart has never been fuller.

chapter eleven

CALLUM
january

Stepping into the doctor's office, I glance around the waiting room for Ellie. She's seated off to the side near the window. The sunshine peeks in through the blinds making her look even more like an angel.

The first trimester was hard on her in several ways. For a while, it started to feel like what happened at Hudson's had set us back to where we were after she was taken by Royal.

The combination of morning sickness, which seemed to happen more than just in the morning, and the lack of sleep from nightmares, made it hard on her body. After we spent some time together and separately talking to her counselor, we found she still has a lot of fear over the thought of losing me and raising our child alone.

In a lot of ways, it resurfaced the same feelings she had when she was younger after her dad died and how difficult it had been to witness the grief her mom went through from his passing. Over the past few weeks, her morning sickness has improved, and she decided it was time for her to go back to work. We hadn't really talked about what she would do when the baby arrived, but I didn't want to push her. If she felt she was ready, I knew it was a big step for her to go back to working at Hudson's. Those steps forward were all I wanted to focus on right now, no matter how hard they may be for the both of us.

She reminded me it was time we focused on all the things we had to be thankful for. I couldn't have agreed with her more.

Ellie glances up from the magazine she was flipping through as the door shuts behind me. When her eyes fall on mine, they light up as her smile grows wide. There's something so sexy about seeing my wife's stomach along with our baby inside her.

She sees me look down at her stomach, as she runs her palm over her shirt.

"Daddy's here," she whispers as I approach, so only the two of us can hear. Rubbing my hand over her stomach, I lean forward and kiss her.

"Of course, I am. Do you think I'd want to miss this?"

There's a flash of guilt on Ellie's face. I know she feels bad I wasn't with her for the first ultrasound. We didn't know she was pregnant or what to expect. When she explained to me how she wanted to be certain it was positive before she told me she was pregnant, I understood why, even though I hated knowing I missed something so important. She didn't want to tell me, get my hopes up, only for it to turn out to be negative. I hate thinking about how this all could've been ripped away from both of us.

Either way, I had to remind her regardless of what came our way, I was always gonna be by her side every step of the way. She promised me we wouldn't have any secrets between us ever again.

"Ellie Reid," the nurse announces into the waiting room and we both stand.

"Oh my gosh, Callum, I'm so excited." There's a nervous giggle in her voice I hear bubble up.

"I am, too," I whisper to her, as I run my palm over her back leading her through the door and down the hallway to the patient room.

"I'm Leddy, I'll be your nurse for today. Do you have any concerns before Doctor Sattler comes in?"

Ellie glances over at me, before looking back at her and shakes her head. "No, we're just really excited for the sonogram."

"I can imagine." She smiles a warm smile, as she approaches Ellie picking up the blood pressure cuff and wrapping it securely around Ellie's arm. I stand next to her, rubbing her back as she goes through the motions of getting her vitals.

"I'll let her know you're ready."

We both thank her as Ellie lies back on the exam room table, running her hands over her stomach. Bending down next to her, I pull up her shirt and press a kiss against her stomach. That's how the doc finds us when she walks into the room a minute later.

We're on a first name basis now, as we've become well acquainted over the past few months. I don't think she understood what I meant when I told her I was going to be very involved with making sure my wife was well cared for during her pregnancy.

"Ellie, Callum. It's good to see you both."

She has a pen tucked behind her ear, as she pulls the chair out facing us both before reading through Ellie's chart.

"How have you been feeling? Has your morning sickness improved? I haven't heard from you both lately."

There's a smirk on the edge of her mouth as her eyes bounce between mine and back to Ellie. There's a not-so-subtle hint she had been receiving one too many phone calls from me. Ellie laughs, her face turning a rosy shade of pink, as she adjusts her shirt and I help her to sit up.

"Much better, thank you for your advice. The past couple of weeks have been a lot better. I'm glad because I couldn't imagine going through the rest of the pregnancy feeling the way I was."

"You're welcome. I'm glad, for both of your sakes, that you're feeling better."

Ellie laughs again, as she pats her hand on my arm, clearly finding my overprotective ways amusing. I went to Everton and nearly bought out the Target store with all the products Doctor Sattler and other experienced moms were suggesting online.

"I'm always going to take care of you," I say matter-of-factly. Ellie's face softens, as I lean forward pressing a kiss to her lips. I don't give a shit I'm kissing her, right here in the exam room in front of our doctor. I don't think Ellie cares either.

Now that we've crossed into the second trimester and she's been feeling better, it's like a switch has been flipped in her. Her need for me is insatiable. It's the fuel to my desire that burns for her always.

The sound of a throat clearing next to me pulls me away from my wife and her lips. Ellie bites her lip, hiding her grin as I flash her a wink.

"Sorry," I say. The grin on my face says I'm not at all sorry.

"I know you're both looking forward to the ultrasound today. Any questions before we begin?"

"Uh... yeah, actually I do have a question. At what point in the pregnancy do I need to worry about sex posing a risk to the baby? I'm not going to hurt anything, am I?"

Ellie coughs, clearly taken off guard by my question. Looking at her, I rub her back making sure she's fine.

Her eyes are wide as she holds her hand up. The look on her face is a mixture of shocked and horrified.

"What?" I ask at the same time she sternly says, "Callum."

"You have nothing to be worried about, Callum. You're not going to hurt Ellie or the baby. Sex during pregnancy is perfectly fine. In fact, it's healthy and encouraged."

"Well thank fuck for that." I laugh. "You hear that baby? She says it's encouraged."

Ellie wraps her hand over her mouth to contain her giggle.

"I'm sorry." She looks back to the doctor.

"It's okay. It wouldn't be the first time I've heard this question and it most certainly won't be the last either."

She pulls the sonogram machine closer to her. "If you're both ready now, I'd love to show you your baby. That way we can make sure everything is going smoothly. Hopefully, if he or she cooperates with us, I can tell you the gender too."

Ellie lies back on the table, getting comfortable. Leaning over her, I press a kiss against her forehead.

The sound of rushing water fills the room, followed by the sound I know as our baby's heartbeat. We've been able to hear the heartbeat on the doppler at every visit I've gone to with Ellie. The rapid beat in my ears slams into me; all my emotions gripping me by the heart.

I'm unsure of what I'm looking at, as the doctor rubs a wand over Ellie's swollen belly.

"Hey there, little one," Doctor Sattler says, as she squirts more jelly on her belly. The picture adjusts as she moves it around again. I'm about to ask her to tell me what I'm looking at when a small face appears on the screen and tears prick the corner of my eyes.

"There he is."

"He?" I ask, wanting to make sure I heard her right.

She moves the wand again. "Yep, it looks like it's a he. He's an active one, squirming around a lot, but he's definitely wanting us to know he's all boy."

Ellie's hand squeezes mine and my eyes flash down at hers. Seeing the tears streaming down her face pushes me over the edge. I can't hold it back any longer.

"It's a boy," she whispers.

"We're going to have a son, sweetheart."

I press a hard kiss against her lips, as I brush her hair away from her face.

We both are enraptured by the sounds of his heartbeat and the images of our baby on the screen. The first time I heard his heartbeat was when it truly clicked into place and it hit me, I was going to be a dad. Seeing his little face today, I start to picture the life we'll have together.

There were times I wondered if we could get to where we are now and if having a family would ever be in the cards for us. We've had more challenges thrown our way than anyone should have to face. I love Ellie more than life itself and I'll spend all my days giving her the same happiness and love she's given me.

epilogue

ELLIE
may

"CALLUM!" I shout from the bathroom in a panic.

"I'm coming!"

I can hear the worry in his voice as he bounds down the hallway toward our room.

The door swings open and his eyes are bright and frantic, whereas mine are full of emotion. I'm on the verge of crying, feeling all the emotions bubbling up inside me.

"You okay, baby?" Callum asks, racing into the room as his eyes look over me.

"Umm... I think my, oh, shit, I think my water just broke." There's a mix of uncertainty and awe in my voice.

He stands there for a moment, almost frozen in place as a smile stretches wide over his face. It's as if it's finally hitting us all at once, it's here. The day is finally here.

I expect Callum to kick it into gear, and patiently rush me around the house to grab our bags and get out the door. He takes me by surprise as he steps in closer to me, dropping to his knees on the floor. I can't help but stare down at him in wonder.

"You ready, sweetheart?"

He presses his hands on either side of my stomach, leaning in and presses a kiss against my round belly.

"I've been counting down the days, Callum. I can't believe it's happening now."

Any of the nerves and anxiety I felt a moment ago lessen, just having Callum near me.

"It's gonna to be okay. I promise I'll be there with you every step of the way."

Tears fill the brims of my eyes. Letting out a deep sigh, I breathe out slowly, which isn't easy to do, trying to hold back the tears as one escapes and streams down the side of my face.

"Don't cry, baby." His voice is smooth and reassuring. "You're too beautiful to cry."

I run my hands over Callum's, where they're pressed lightly against the sides of my tummy.

"Alright, buddy! This is it," he says to my tummy. "It's the day we've been training for the past several months. Now I know you're excited, you want to make your debut, but let me get your momma to the hospital safely, then you can rock 'n roll."

This has become a regular occurrence for us lately, where he spends time talking to me and our son. He likes to talk to him as if he were here, and I can't help but love hearing all the stories he tells him.

Callum stands, tangling his fingers in my hair as he presses a kiss against my lips and once more on my forehead.

"You go get your shoes on and grab your purse. I'll get the bag and meet you at the door."

I've dreamt about this day happening, about seeing Callum's face the moment we both meet our son. Callum holds my hand the entire way to the hospital. He kisses the back, reassuring me it is all going to be okay.

A lot has changed over the past few months, but in the best way possible. Shortly after we found out we were having a boy, Callum surprised me with a trip back to my hometown, Garwood. He didn't tell me about it until the day we left. A part of him worried it would set back my progress.

The trip ended up being the best thing for the both of us and our healing. For me, it was an opportunity to show Callum were I was from. I took him by the cemetery where my dad and Grams were both buried. They were the two most important people in my life before I met Callum. They are the reason I had the courage to leave Garwood in the first place and, had that not have happened, I know I wouldn't have found Callum either.

For a long time, it felt like I was running away from the past but being able to go back there helped me finally see how far I've come. I'm so grateful Callum took me on the trip. It gave me a sense of closure I had been searching for.

There was no preparing me for the moment I held my son for the first time. Sitting in the hospital bed as I stare down as his precious face and feel his soft skin against mine, I'm reminded of all the good there is in the world as a feeling of contentment washes over me.

"He has your nose," Callum whispers, sitting on the edge of the bed with one arm wrapped around me and the other helping cradle our son.

"He does." I smile, leaning forward to press a kiss against his cheek.

"You want to hold him?" I ask, glancing up at Callum.

"Oh boy, do I ever." He grins, leaning closer to slide his arms underneath mine. Callum takes over, standing near me at the hospital bed as he bounces him in his arms. His face is pressed in close to our son's, whispering softly to him before he pulls back and says, "Yeah, buddy. She's beautiful, isn't she? She's also the strongest and most loving woman I know. We're two of the luckiest guys in the world."

"You look good holding our son, Daddy." I grin, as Callum leans over to press a kiss against my forehead.

"Mm, I like the way that sounds coming from you." He winks. "Think you're gonna have to give me a few more of these, baby."

"I'm holding you to that," I sigh, leaning back as I watch my husband pace around the room as he kisses him on the forehead before he starts talking to him once again.

"You hear that, Liam? I think you're going to have a little brother or sister soon."

All I've ever wanted was for us to have a family and grow old together. Our road to where we are now wasn't always easy. But watching Callum hold our son, I know I'm where I'm meant to be. I've found the love I've been searching for and now that I found him, I'm finally home.

Thank you for reading **NOW THAT I FOUND YOU**! I hope you love catching up with Callum and Ellie's as much as I did.

You can continue the Heart's Compass series with Where You Belong. It's about a single mom breaking free from an abusive marriage, finding love with the small-town cop, who happens to be Corbin Reid. That's right, Callum and Ellie's son has his own story!

You can sign up for my newsletter to learn more about my new releases. You can also join my Facebook group, Brooke O'Brien's Rebel Reader Group, for exclusive giveaways and sneak peeks of future books. To join, visit:

www.authorbrookeobrien.com/follow.

Now, turn the page for a sneak peek of Where You Belong...

WHERE *you belong*

A HEART'S COMPASS
BOOK FIVE

USA TODAY BESTSELLING AUTHOR
BROOKE O'BRIEN

prologue

HAELYNN

I've stared at the same text on my phone for the past thirty minutes. The dread filling the pit of my stomach is insurmountable. The darkness of the room nearly swallows me whole.

Sometimes I feel like I'm living two different lives.

During the day, I put on a brave face for my son. He's the only thing I have in my life to keep me going, and I fight every day to keep from burdening him with my pain.

When he drifts off to sleep, the sinking depression I've managed to keep at bay during the day threatens to break the barrier until nothing is left to fend it off.

I rub my fingers over my face. My hair falls around me like a curtain, and I continue my path, pushing them through the strands and gripping them in my fist.

Every night I sit here, overwhelmed by the impending moment when he'll come home, and I have nowhere left to run. Nowhere to hide.

Headlights flash through the window, and unease twists in my stomach like a knot. In the distance, I hear the faint sound of the garage door open, mixed with the steady beat of my heart hammering in my chest.

Tears fill the brim of my eyes, and my lips quiver as I fight to keep my emotions bottled up tight. I squeeze my eyes shut as a teardrop lands on my cheek and streaks down my face. I quickly swipe the palm of my hand over my damp skin and let out a heavy exhale.

It will get better. One day, it will get better.

I've repeated those words to myself so many times, I'm beginning to wonder if I believe them to be true or if I'm trying to will myself there.

The door leading from the garage into the house slams shut with force and jolts me from my thoughts. My hand pats around on the bathroom rug, searching for my phone to check the baby monitors to see if Huxton woke up from the noise.

Atlas is in one of his moods. I could sense it from the clipped responses in his text he sent me earlier tonight. As expected, he couldn't care less about the fact our son should be sleeping in the bedroom next to ours.

Huxton is fast asleep in bed with his little arm draped above his head. His soft snores are drowned out by the white noise machine. When enough time has passed without him moving or crying, I'm convinced the door slamming didn't wake him.

My husband is the reason I dread putting my son to bed. I know when I do, I'm only another minute away from when he'll walk through the door.

In the early part of our marriage, I spent so much time trying to convince him to come home earlier. I tried telling him how much I missed him, how hard it was doing it alone when he'd be gone anywhere from ten to twelve hours a day only to come home, eat, and go straight to bed.

In the beginning, he tried, but as the days went by, it started happening more and more until we were back to where we started. I've spent so much time crying, practically begging him to put us first.

I have no more energy left.

I can make out the faint sound of his footsteps coming up the stairs. I squeeze my eyes shut, wishing he'd change his clothes and go to sleep. I press the palms of my hands against my eyes, saying a prayer he'll leave me alone tonight.

When his footsteps draw near, I blink through the tears forming beneath the crack of the door. He doesn't bother knocking, reaching for the doorknob only to find it locked.

"You gonna lock me out of my own fucking bath-room?"

"I'm getting ready to take a bath," I lie.

It's not like it's a stretch, though. If it'll give me space from him, I'll do what I need to do. Sometimes I'll slip in here when he gets home, light some candles, and turn on soothing music to try to relax enough to fall asleep.

"Open the door." His stern voice sends chills up my spine.

I stand, hitting the light switch above the bathtub. It's soft, muted, and less harsh on my eyes. If he knew I was sitting here in the dark, he'd ask questions, and I don't think either of us is ready for the truth of my answers.

My eyes are red and bloodshot from crying. I do a quick swipe under my eye and try to shake the dread eating me up inside. I flip the lock and open the door as he pushes into the space.

His tall frame towers over me. He leans against the doorframe, his eyes roaming over my body, narrowing when they meet my face. The scent of alcohol on his breath wafts through the air.

It takes everything in me to fend off the urge to curl my lip in disgust at the thought of him driving home, further proving his selfishness.

"C'mere," he drawls, reaching his hand out toward me.

My body goes rigid. He rears his head back, staring down at me. The look on his face says it all. He can't believe I'd have the audacity to recoil from his touch.

"I said come here," he orders.

I take a step toward him, closing the distance between us. I force myself through the movements, pressing my hand against his chest. Despite our proximity, it doesn't escape my notice how distant we feel from one another.

He's no longer the man I married.

My heart doesn't race when he kisses me. My breath doesn't get caught in my throat when he touches me or looks at me from across the room. I don't even remember the last time we kissed or made love, let alone felt an ounce of passion behind it when we did.

My heart aches at the thought of living like this forever, of our son growing up and not seeing love between his parents.

"I'm fuckin' sick of you pulling away from me whenever I try to touch you. What kind of wife are you? Don't you understand I have needs?"

My eyes narrow, and unlike my restraint a moment ago, I don't attempt to shield my disgust. My lip curls, and I shake my head, but I'm not the least bit surprised.

"Why don't you ask yourself the same question, Atlas? What would make you think I'd want to be touched by you?"

His nostrils flare, and his face reddens with anger. His large hand pushes against my chest, and the force behind it sends my body crashing against the door-frame, causing me to cry out in agony.

"You need to remember who the fuck yer talkin' to, do you hear me? If yer not gonna let me fuck you, I'll have no problem findin' someone who will."

His words are jumbled together from the alcohol in his bloodstream.

He shoves his forearm against my chest, and my body collapses on the floor, recoiling from him and his touch. The look of revulsion on his face as he stands over me in a display of dominance lets me know it could've been much worse.

"Leave me alone," I spit out.

He clenches his jaw, shaking his head.

"Now, Atlas. I'm not fuckin' kidding anymore. I'm done! Leave. Me. Alone."

It's the first time I've ever uttered those words to him. The red-hot rage was apparent on his face.

"Who do you think you are turnin' me down? You'd be nothin' without me, you hear me? You'd have noth-in'! If you try to leave me or take my son from me, I'll make your life hell. You understand?"

I never knew what hell was until I met him.

chapter one

HAELYNN
ten months earlier

I guess I'd consider myself superstitious. You'll never find me walking under a ladder, crossing the path of a black cat, and if I see a penny on the ground, I will always stop to pick it up.

These days, I could use all the help I can get regarding a stroke of good luck.

I never expected at twenty-four years old I'd be packing up my life in a couple of hours while my husband was at work to take our son and move us to Arbor Creek.

I've spent the past four years married to a man who no longer resembled the one I fell in love with. People change as they grow older. We go through hard times, and each lesson learned makes us wiser.

Hell, if I'm being honest, I don't think I recognize the woman I see in the mirror either. I can't fault him for changing, but I blame him for the darkness he showed me as time passed.

I saw my opportunity to get out, and I ran like hell while I had the chance.

They say bad luck comes in threes. It started with finding out our dog had to be put down when a tumor in her spine ruptured to learning Atlas started the process of filing bankruptcy without ever telling me. The icing on the cake was finding out all those late nights at the office included stops by the strip club.

I was a stay-at-home mom to our son. Who knew that was the place where businessmen met up to talk about investments?

If the old wives' tale is true, I'm due for some good luck to show up.

After leaving Huxton with my mom this morning, I made the quiet drive across town to our new house and let myself soak in how right this moment had felt.

The first few weeks after we moved out weren't easy. We stayed with my mom for a couple of months, long enough to get back on my feet. I was eager for a place to call my own, though. With enough to cover our first month's rent and a little to fall back on, I took the leap.

If I didn't want to get in over my head, I needed to start looking for a job quickly.

Arbor Creek is a small town in Iowa. It's not far outside of Everton, which makes it the perfect place for me to raise Huxton, but it also makes it difficult to find a job. Securing employment is next on my list after I get settled.

A handful of boxes are left in the back of my mom's rusted old pickup truck. Sweat dots my brow from the summer sun blazing overhead. I lift the sleeve of my T-shirt and dab it across my forehead, exhaling a deep breath before hoisting another box into my arms.

My sneakers squeak against the hardwood floor leading down the hallway, and I drop the box on the island in the center of the kitchen. I dust my hands off and swipe the sweat off my face once more as the sound of glass shattering halts my movement.

"Oh no, no, no!" I wince, finding two of the four wineglasses I just bought now broken on the floor. Of course, it happened right after I cleaned off the counters and swept the floor too.

My phone starts ringing as I'm sweeping the last of the broken shards into my dustpan. "Mom" flashes on the screen, and I swipe to answer the call.

"How are things going?"

"It's going well…" I trail off, resting my hip against the counter while staring at the two remaining glasses. "Or it was until a minute ago, when I accidentally broke some glass on the floor."

"What happened?" she asks, her voice growing concerned.

"I knocked a few glasses off the counter. It's not a big deal."

"Good." She sighed, causing my brows to furrow in confusion. "They say breaking glass in your new home is a sign of evil leaving your house, and good things are coming your way."

Something is oddly comforting about hearing those words right now.

"Well, I'll let you get back to work. When you're ready for us, let me know. We'll bring you some lunch."

We hung up after I told her I only had a few boxes left, and I was going to call it a day once I finished unpacking the kitchen. It wouldn't take long, considering we didn't have much. We didn't need much, though, either.

I knew when we left it wouldn't go over well with Atlas. He'd show remorse, tell me how sorry he was, and offer me the moon with all his meaningless promises. When that didn't work, he'd try to prove I was making a mistake and resort to begging.

I couldn't stand the thought of being stuck in an unhappy marriage for another day. If it took walking away from everything I owned and starting over, it was what I'd do. As long as I have Huxton, I have everything we need.

Everything else will come with time.

After hanging up with my mom, I put in another order at Target for pickup to get a replacement set of wineglasses. I would need those. Then I was back to work.

I hitch my leg up on the tailgate and climbed up into the bed of the truck, pushing the remaining boxes to the edge.

"Hey, neighbor," a friendly voice calls from behind me as I lift one of the boxes. I turn to see who it is, damn near tripping over my own feet. She jogs across the street toward me as I right myself again.

"Need a hand?" She laughs. She's taller, with long blond hair and a bright smile. She waves over her shoulder at the man behind her. The way he smiles at her is full of love, and she grins right back at him.

They are both dressed like they just got in a workout.

"I'm Madelyn." The girl smiles and extends her hand out to me. She points at the guy over her shoulder. "This is my boyfriend, Alex."

"It's nice to meet you," I say, dropping the box on the tailgate. "I'm Haelynn. I'll be living here with my son, Huxton."

Her smile softens at the mention of Huxton.

"I saw the 'For Rent' sign come down earlier this week and have been keeping an eye out for our new neighbors. It looks like you got most of it handled, but can we help with anything?"

"I would appreciate it." I smile. It's only a few more boxes, but the sooner I can wrap this up, the quicker I can finish unpacking the kitchen.

Alex sidesteps her and reaches for one of the boxes. Madelyn and I trail him, and I lead the way into the house. Madelyn follows me into my room with our two boxes while Alex deposits the one in Huxton's room.

"This is such a cute place," she gushes. "I've been looking forward to the day we welcome more people our age to the neighborhood. It's overrun with retired folks, which is great when raising a family in a quiet area, but like I said, it's so quiet."

"You only say that because you're still ticked at Mary Jean for calling Corbin when you were playing your music so loud."

She rolled her eyes. "It was the Fourth of July!"

Alex chuckled, squeezing her shoulder, and muttered, "I know, Penny girl. I know."

She smirked back at him and turned back toward me. "If you're not playing music, grilling out in your backyard, and lighting some sparklers, are you even American?"

I grinned, recalling all the memories of us doing the same growing up.

"She's got a point."

"You'll have to come over and hang with us sometime. Are you from the area originally?"

Over the years, I started to lose touch with the friends I had when I was younger. The thought of making new ones, especially so close by, has me thinking about what my mom said on the phone a little bit ago.

"My mom is from the area, but she moved out of town when she was pregnant with me. I was raised near Chicago but moved back to Everton a few years ago with my ex-husband to raise our son closer to family."

It is the first time I have spoken the word "ex" out loud to anyone since our separation. It feels strange rolling off my tongue.

She nodded, a look of sympathy passing over her face. "I'm from the area myself, but only moved in here with this guy a couple of months ago."

"It took a lot of cajoling, but I persuaded her to give me a chance. Once she did, she didn't want to let me go, so I convinced her to move in with me. I've got too much space for one person anyway." Alex chuckled.

"Yeah, it took a lot of persuasion." Madelyn smirks.

Something about the devilish smiles on their faces has me thinking they enjoyed whatever that entailed.

"I recently opened a photo studio in town, just down off Fallon Street. If you and Huxton would like family photos, I'll hook you up with a good deal."

My heart warmed at the thought of getting pictures taken with Huxton, just the two of us.

The mention of a photo studio in town spurred a thought after perusing job postings last night.

"Photo studio? You wouldn't happen to be talking about the one..." I pause, snapping my fingers in hopes it will help me remember the name of the place I bookmarked to my favorites. "Is it Memories and Moments?"

She smiles. "That's me!"

"I saw the posting online for an assistant. I was planning on applying this weekend."

"Are you kidding? What a small world." She smiles, her eyes lighting up. "I'll give you my number and when things settle down this weekend, shoot me a text message and we can chat more about the position. I'm looking to have someone start soon, so if you're interested, the sooner the better."

"That would be perfect. Huxton starts school next week, and I'm ready to get myself back out there."

She grins. "We can make that happen!"

Alex ducks out a few minutes later after assuring me he'll be around if I need a handyman. Madelyn stuck around after he left, chatting with me and lending a hand while we unpacked the kitchen.

She talked about how she and Alex met. He was from a small town in Wisconsin but met through mutual friends when he came to visit for a few weeks over the summer. They had spent every available second together, but when the time came for him to go back home, she wasn't ready to let him go.

Atlas and I did the long-distance thing for a while when he moved back to Everton and I was still in school. I know how hard it can be on a relationship, especially when you don't have your future all mapped out together.

Chatting with Madelyn brings back memories of my friends from Chicago. I made a mental note to reach out to them.

I can't shake how early this morning I had a good feeling things were around the corner. In a span of a couple of hours, not only did I make a new friend but I also had a job opportunity all but fall in my lap.

This is the start of the next chapter in my life, and for the first time in a long time, I'm excited about what the future has in store.

chapter two

HAELYNN

"All right, Huxie, you have fun with Gram, and I'll see you when I get off work."

He drops his toy truck on the floor from where he's standing in the middle of my mom's double-wide trailer and runs toward me, his arms flying around my waist, squeezing me in a hug.

This week has been big for the two of us.

"I love you, sweetie," I whisper, crouching down to wrap my arms around his small body. His dark hair and chocolate eyes reach into my chest and squeeze my heart.

Everything I do in life is for this boy, and I'd walk away from my marriage countless times if it meant keeping him safe.

"I love you too." His words are muffled from his small cheek pressed against the side of my arm.

He pulls back, lands a kiss against my cheek, and flashes me a huge grin before darting off to the living room.

The sound of my mom's heavy cough echoes down the hall. She strolls toward me, hair disheveled on one side and a large cup of coffee in her hand, evident she rolled out of bed not long ago.

"Quit worrying about the boy. He's with me, so he'll be fine. I did a decent enough job of raisin' you, didn't I? Now get outta here. Let me spend time with my grandson."

I exhale a chuckle and nod in agreement.

"I should be here just after four. I googled the address, and it's not too far from here."

"Of course it's not far. This is Arbor Creek. What did you expect? Now, go!"

I peer over at Huxton, but he's too busy lining up his toy cars to pay me any mind, so I sneak out the door, leaving them be.

Madelyn texted me last night to run through everything I'd need to know before my first day. We had talked off and on over the weekend. I couldn't believe how quickly we clicked.

The opportunity to work with her has come at the perfect time. I need a job as desperately as she desires an assistant. We covered more about what the position entailed. I'll be taking over scheduling appointments and running her social media, helping keep things running smoothly so she could focus her time and attention on all things photography.

She gushed over an idea she saw scrolling on TikTok and asked me if I'd help her with it. She didn't give me many details, just told me to bring some fall-inspired clothes and leave the rest up to her.

Although I have no idea what I am getting myself into, I know this is her baby, and she won't steer me wrong.

The GPS signals for me to turn right onto Fallon Street. A strip of businesses lines the main street leading into the small two-block downtown area. I spot Memories and Moments on the end and pull into the small parking area on the side street, leaving the space open in the front for customers passing by.

Iron lanterns hang against the dark brick building, giving off a cozy rustic vibe. The doorbell dings when I pull the door open, and the scent of coconut swirls through the air. The studio is open in the front, with a large desk in the center of the room separating the waiting area from the rest of the space.

There are candles lit along the counter, and soft music plays overhead. Something about the energy of the studio fits, and I feel right at home.

Madelyn peeks her head out of a doorway near the far back, her larger-than-life smile spreads across her face.

"Haelynn," she sings. "Oh my gosh, you're here!" She waves frantically, dashing toward me. "I'm so excited. Are you excited? I hope you are!"

Any hesitation or worry I may have been holding on to is gone when I see how happy she is. Her smile and personality are infectious.

"Very! It was hard to leave Huxton this morning, but we need this. I need this!" I press my palm to my chest, emphasizing how much I mean it.

She bounces on her feet, clapping her hands. Her eyes look from mine down to the bag in my hand.

"Oh good, you brought everything with you." She smiles, motioning for me to follow her.

There's a bed pushed against the wall, and a backdrop directly across from it with a wicker folding screen toward the back, likely where her clients go for wardrobe changes.

"Corbin should be here any minute. You'll love him. This will turn out perfect," she gushes.

My brows furrow as I'm pulling clothes out of my bag, laying them out to show Madelyn. I pause, wondering who the heck Corbin is?

"Does he work for you too?"

When we had spoken, she led me to believe she's been working here and running the studio by herself.

"No, he's a friend of mine. He's coming for the photo shoot." She motions her hand toward the clothes, seemingly confused by my question.

"Did you get the TikTok video I sent you last night?"

I shake my head.

"Oh, well, that makes sense." She chuckles. "It's for a stranger photo shoot. I got the idea from another photographer on TikTok. Here, let me show you."

She reaches for her phone in her back pocket. Pulling it out, she scrolls with her finger while my heart starts hammering in my chest.

She wants me to do a photo shoot with this… Corbin, and we've never even met.

I shake out my hands, trying to formulate the words to break this to her, but I don't think I'm the right person for the shoot. The guilt twisting in the pit of my stomach leaves me feeling uneasy.

This is my first day. I haven't even made it more than ten minutes, and I'm already disappointing Madelyn.

"Here it is." She grins, turning the phone toward me. It takes me a second to even focus on the screen. The video shows clips of two couples meeting for the first time and their various poses during the shoot.

You can see the connection between the two strangers even in the short video, and the anxious feeling of being able to give her the same makes my body tremble.

I shove the fears aside, though. Despite the worry of being unable to deliver, I'm an expert at covering up my emotions and putting on a brave face to prevent anyone around me from knowing how I feel.

"Wow, you can feel the connection between them. That's amazing!"

"Right?" Madelyn sighs, reaching for the phone to watch the video clip again before slipping it back into her pocket. "I thought it was a good idea to add to my collection of work and maybe entice some new clients to book their upcoming event with me. Anything will help, right?"

I didn't want to let her down by telling her how I haven't been touched by another man in over a year. Hell, it's been even longer since I was intimate with Atlas.

I'm not sure I can evoke the same emotions watching that clip, but I'll give my best effort.

She looks over the outfits I brought with me and assures me they'll be perfect.

"Oh, he's here!" she squeals. "You should get changed. Let me know when you're ready, and I'll walk you out, so we can start with the initial meeting. Does that sound good?"

I bite my lower lip, trying to stop the words on the tip of my tongue from slipping out. It's not that I don't want to do this or that I can't do this; it's more that I don't want to disappoint Madelyn.

She's been wonderful to me since we first met, and the last thing I want to do is to let her down.

I scoop the clothes in my arms and slip behind the divider to change.

"Oh, I left the mask to cover your eyes on the hook in the corner. Do you see it?"

"Yes," I croak out. "Yes, I do."

Standing in the mirror, I stare at the girl looking back at me. My mind flashes back to the nights I'd slip away to the bathroom, desperately seeking distance from him. I'd get lost in my mind staring at my reflection, thinking about how I ended up here and dreaming about the day when I'd break free. I was constantly walking on eggshells around him, and every second he was home began to feel like a countdown until the moment he would leave.

It dawns on me, taking in the look on my face, how different I look from the woman I saw a year ago.

The lost look I saw in my eyes doesn't look so distant, and the dark circles under my eyes have begun to fade away. My cheeks are fuller, and the sun-kissed tan highlighting my skin glows, reminding me of all the good things coming my way.

Something about seeing this change right now, on the brink of starting a new chapter in my life, has me letting out a heavy sigh of relief. It's the sign I needed, reminding me of how much change I've gone through and how many risks I've taken to get here.

The door dinging in the distance yanks me from my thoughts, pulling me right back into the present.

"Well, look who it is," Madelyn sings.

"Hey, darlin'." Something about his deep, raspy tone zips like lightning through my body, causing my stom-ach to flip.

I slip my shirt over my head, folding and setting it in a pile on the chair, leaving on the white tank top I'm wearing underneath.

"Thank you again for doing this for me."

"It's no problem. It's not like you had a lot of options. I can't imagine you wanting Alex to step in, and we both know it would take an act of God to convince Gage to do anything like this."

Madelyn laughs. "You're not lying."

I pull over the burgundy top, adjusting the cinched band around my waist. The sleeves are less fitted, flowing over my arms.

"I can't believe I let you convince me, though. Who wants pictures of me with a stranger?" He chuckles. "Although you did promise me she was beautiful, so how could I say no?"

Something about knowing he's nervous but was looking forward to meeting me is oddly comforting. I trust Madelyn, and although she doesn't know a lot about me or my past, I don't think she'd associate with a man she didn't trust.

I pull on my jeans, sitting snug on my hips, and step back into the booties I wore for my first day.

"How are you doing over there, Haelynn?"

A throat clears, and he mutters, "You coulda warned me she was listening."

I cover my mouth to contain my laughter.

"Give me just a second to get this mask on, and I'll be ready."

"You need to get your mask on too. Here," Madelyn says. "Now stand over here."

I picture her leading him to where she wants him.

The floorboards creak with footsteps walking toward me, and Madelyn's head peeks around the divider.

"Good choice! You look great," she whispers.

I shake out my hands, and she murmurs under her breath. "Don't be nervous. Corbin's one of the sweetest men I know, and you'll be great together. I promise!"

I rub my lips together, the gloss I put on earlier still coating them, pulling the mask over my face to cover my eyes. Madelyn slides her arm into mine, guiding me into the studio with her. The floorboards creak beneath us, and Andrew Jannakos plays through the speakers around us. I know when I get closer to Corbin, judging by the woodsy scent mixed with the clean smell of laundry detergent lingering in the air. It's a distinct smell that's all male.

Madelyn turns me to face the other direction and mutters for me not to move so she can grab her camera. I wring my hands out, rubbing them on the front of my jeans.

"Okay, I'm ready when you are."

I slip my mask off my face, blinking to adjust my eyes to the lighting, and glance over at Madelyn. She's ready and waiting, snapping pictures. The camera covers most of her face, but you can't miss her large grin as the camera clicks away.

I turn, and my eyes fall on Corbin, taking in the soft caramel of his eyes. Something about the sparkle mixed with the curve of his smile has me breaking out in a grin of my own.

"Goddamn, she wasn't lying. You are more than beautiful, you are... I don't even know the word."

His hands reach out toward me, pulling me into his arms. I toss my head back, a genuine laugh bubbling up from inside me, shaking my head.

"I'm not sure, but you sure know how to sweet-talk a woman, don't you?"

"Did it work?" He smirks. My hands glide over the tight ridges of his chest, my fingers gripping his shirt to pull him closer to me.

I forget Madelyn is in the room with us and drown out the sound of the shutter clicking with each picture she takes.

It's like everything around us falls away, and it's only the two of us. Any other time, I'd be second-guessing my every move, ruining the moment by analyzing every moment.

Not today. I'm rolling with it.

I'm seizing the day.

Do you want more Corbin & Haelynn?

Check out Where You Belong today at:
www.authorbrookeobrien.com/whereyoubelong

BOOKS BY BROOKE

A Rebels Havoc Series

Brix
Sins of a Rebel
Tysin
Trey
Madden

Men of Blaze

Personal Foul
Reckless Rebound (Cocky Hero Club)

Tattered Heart Duet

Torn
Tattered

A Heart's Compass Series

Where I Found You
Lost Before You
Until I Found You
Now That I Found You

Where You Belong

Standalones (In order of publication)

Wild Irish

Learn more and purchase your copy at:
www.authorbrookeobrien.com/booksbybrooke

ABOUT BROOKE

USA Today Bestselling author Brooke O'Brien writes steamy and swoon-worthy new adult romances. She's best known for her sports and rock star romances.

Brooke believes a love worth having is worth fighting for, and she brings this into her stories where her characters risk it all for love.

When she isn't writing or falling in love with a new book boyfriend, you can find her spending time with her family, cheering on her favorite sports teams, listening to ASMR, or binge-watching the latest true crime documentary. She loves rockin' a comfy hoodie with leggings and believes the best days include a good nap.

Brooke loves connecting with readers and hopes you'll join her on her social pages or reader group to stay in touch. To follow Brooke and join her newsletter, visit authorbrookeobrien.com/follow.

ACKNOWLEDGMENTS

My Boys – I love you more than anything on this earth. Everything I do is for our family.

Mom, Gram, & Ash – Thanks for always being supportive of this journey. You've pushed me to go after everything I want in life. Love you!

To my AMAZING beta readers – Elizabeth, Ana, Ashley, and Cheryl. Thank you for reading Graham & Halle's story before anyone else, for your honest feedback, and helping me make their story better. I'm so grateful for you! <3

My Rebels Babes – I love being able to connect with all of you in my Reader Group. I feel like I've found a place where I can share with you my triumphs and crazy ideas, as well as catching up with you about everything going on in our daily lives. I'm so grateful to have all your support. To my Release Launch Rebels, thank you for being a part of this one.

Kate Jessop – What would I do without you? I don't want to find out. Thank you for being there for me when I need to brainstorm an idea or tell me it's going to be okay when I need to hear it.

Ana Quinn – I'm giving you two shout outs because YOU DESERVE IT. Thank you for being there for me, for listening when I need it, for checking in and pushing me when I need the extra shove in the right direction.

Melissa Pötgens – Girl, I'm so thankful for you. You've stuck by me since the beginning, cheering me on every step of the way and loving my characters as much as I do. Thank you for being you. For EVERYTHING!

My editor, Roxane LeBlanc. I always enjoy working with you. Thank you for being honest, patient, and so very helpful to me.

My proofreader, Julie Deaton. You have a fantastic eye for detail, and I appreciate all your help in getting this book polished off. Thank you for everything!

Najla with Najla Qamber Designs, you are so incredibly talented and blow me away with your work. Thank you for designing the most beautiful cover.

To Ena with Enticing Journey, thank you for your support and helping me promote my work. I'm forever grateful!

Lastly, to all the fantastic bloggers and authors who have shown me support throughout this journey. I hope you know how grateful I am for every one of you.

COPYRIGHT

Now That I Found You: A Heart's Compass novella
Copyright © 2019 by Brooke O'Brien with Tattered Ink
Publishing
All Rights Reserved

No part of this book may be reproduced or transmitted in any form or by any means, electronic or mechanical, including photocopying, recording, or by any information storage and retrieval system without written permissions of the author, except for the use of brief quotations in a review.

This is a work of fiction. Names, characters, places and incidents either are the product of the author's imagination or are used fictitiously. Any resemblance to persons, living or dead, business establishments, events, or locales is entirely coincidental. The author acknowledges the trademarked status and trademark owners of various products referenced in this work of fiction, which has been used without permission. The publication/use of these trademarks is not authorized, associated with or sponsored by the trademark owners.

For information on subsidiary rights, please contact Tattered Ink Publishing at www.authorbrookeobrien.com.